THE HOLE IN THE RABBIT

When a New York City reality show producer and mother of three, is blacklisted from the entertainment industry and then brutally attacked, a spiraling addiction and a taunting accident from her past resurface old wounds, illuminating a history of violence and its damaging inheritance.

By Amy Sewell

ISBN-979-8-9991888-0-9

Cover design & interior layout by: Samantha Sewell

Legal Disclaimer

This is a work of fiction. Unless otherwise indicated, all the names, characters, businesses, places, events and incidents in this book are either the product of the author's imagination or used in a fictitious manner. Any resemblance to the actual persons, living or dead, or actual events is purely coincidental.

The Hole in the Rabbit
Reviews:

A razor sharp, exquisitely personal descent into addiction and the effects of lifelong trauma. The Hole in the Rabbit takes us on a ride that shocks - mainly because of how connected we are to Grace, and how we frequently see ourselves in a character that's making all the wrong choices in her life. I couldn't put it down - an excellent read!

~ Marilyn Agrelo

Captivating with its unflinching, painfully real portrayal of a woman, a mother, who could be any of us with hidden traumas or long-held secrets. Complex and raw, navigating a journey that feels both deeply personal and universally relatable. Struggles with addiction, the past, and the painful decisions faced are delivered with such nuance that I couldn't help but feel the weight of her choices. Both a haunting and eye-opening look at how unspoken childhood wounds and the sacrifices we make for family can shape, and sometimes shatter, our lives, makes for a truly powerful read.

~ Barbara Guest

The Hole in the Rabbit continues the gifted Amy Sewell's exploration of the hidden violence in everyday lives that she began in her first novel, Pocket8s. Secrets and gnawing emptiness lay at our cores in America and Sewell explores these themes with complex, fascinating characters. Sewell is on a mission, and I suggest you join her. You will learn important truths about yourself.

~ Laurel Brett,
author of *The Schrödinger Girl*

This is a gripping story of a woman wrestling with demons she long thought she had under control while grappling with the gray areas of silent trauma often presented, or disguised, as addiction.

~ Heather Ogilvie Stone,
author of *Alternatives to Abstinence: A New Look at Alcoholism and the Choices in Treatment*

This book is dedicated to everyone who has a hole and hasn't been able to fill it.

PART I
Heritance
Downers Grove, Illinois. 1970s

1

THE CAR COMES around the corner faster than it can handle. Screeching. Goodyears burning skid marks into the road. Our heads, as if on bobbing pivots, swivel fast, and our bodies trail in slow motion, jackknifing any and all ability to maneuver quickly, if at all. We are able to do absolutely nothing but be stormed by the old clunker of a car, bouncing like a boat on shallow-troughed whitecaps, ferrying neighborhood hoodlums. The driver regains control in enough time to come to an alarming halt, shaking the chassis and shuddering the rusted steel panels that pass for coupe doors.

The barrel of the gun suddenly lifts, cocks, steadies, and aims.

CLICK.

"BANG!" someone yells.

We throw our bodies directly backward, vertically, propelled by a self-imagined force, blasted down by a firehouse hose. Our limbs flap out front, too late to the game, rag dolls riveted by bullets (that never come). Our tail bones hit earth first, our heads whipping back and then forward. Once down, we strain to prop onto our elbows, to witness our last breaths, and to take note of who took them from within the big ol' turd of a car.

Laughter. *Laughter?* Loud, horrifying, bullying, bold, forced cackles come from the car.

Wind-knocked torsos, our tailbones hold hostage a stinging pain until we think the "coast is clear." Our ears ring, dizzy, nauseous. Our bodies splay out, legs sprawl wide, chests up and out. Our retinas fight to focus, focus, focus.

The blur clears—four panting, shaggy-haired heads, their mouths wide open. Each with its own collection of crooked teeth stands as a monument to trouble and slow decay in all ways.

They grin. They laugh. *Laughing.*

"Motherfu. . ." Pam exhales, out of breath. All that comes out of me is a short gasp of air, hardly enough for my inhale to help me catch my breath.

"Pussies! Look at the pussies!" one of the idiots blurts out.

"Fuck yeah," another idiot confirms.

"Fuck you," Pam hammers back.

"Fuck YOU!" comes back from the first idiot.

"Motherfucker," Pam says as she leans forward and begins to crawl methodically on all fours. Panting. Panting. Panting. "Do . . . you. . . know. . . who my motherfucking brother is?" she hisses out as she stalks toward the car, a lioness approaching prey.

"Holy shit, step on it!" says Idiot #1.

"Fuck! Johnny's. . . it's. . ." says Idiot #2.

"Ha!" Idiot #3, in the passenger front side seat, laughs. "No, no, don't go. Let's see what she does."

"Come on Scott! Don't mess around!" says Idiot #2.

Pam is getting closer. Her red, frizzy hair appears to light up and then expand out, resembling the hairs that stand up on the back of a dog when threatened. Her green eyes narrow, locking in, collecting info.

"Nah, you come on. Now who's the pussy?" laughs Idiot #3, who we discover is "Scott," the one who shot the gun.

"Aw shit, man," says Idiot #1.

The driver is silent, unruffled, and amused, his jet-black hair and dark eyes holding court above his very precise and well-cared-for Fu Manchu. More detached than the others, he watches Pam out of the corner of his eyes. He keeps the car idling.

A couple of feet from the car, Pam stands up, placing her hands on her hips as she begins to take a mental inventory. Pam earned herself a bit of a reputation as a crazy bitch and her older brother John, most definitely as one bad dude—not to be messed with. Johnny ruled the West Side. When he dropped out of high school, he became a culinary kid-wonder at a local hotspot, but even this remained a side hustle, second to the much more lucrative and exciting world of cocaine.

I am no living angel, and I have cache due to my brothers, (mostly Billy) and my sassy sister, Marilyn. Where Pam has balls, I have restraint. I hold back to calculate the situation, as I am all too well aware that things can flare south awfully fast, so I try to err on the side of calm and cool.

"Let's see, we have Scott and Dean. Hey Dean," Pam addresses the driver. Dean gives her a nod. Scott smiles at such an intimate exchange embellished with mutual respect.

She continues, "Idiot #1 in the back is Steve? Steve Grayden? Am I right? And you," she says pointing to Idiot #2, ". . . you're Beth's brother, right? Rich? Rich Kessler?

"It's cool, Pammy," Scott says.

"Is it Scott? Is it?" asks Pam.

"All good fun," says Scott.

"What?" asks Pam.

"Good fun. It's not loaded," Scott says. He waves the gun around, back and forth, his way of gesturing it is not loaded.

Pam turns to look at me, a literal red line of flush flowing up and through her face, from chin to hairline.

"Jesus Christ. You're fucking kidding me," she mumbles, shaking her head in disbelief. "It's not loaded! It's not loaded!" She mimics Scott in a whiny voice. Pam turns back to the bandits, hands even more firmly planted, her nails digging into her pelvic bones, "That's really fucked up. F-u-c-k-e-d UP!"

"Ah, come on. It was nothing Pammy," Scott purrs.

"You're still gonna pay," Pam seethes.

"I'm sure I will. Just not now. Not today. Johnny doesn't need to know. . ." Scott replies with an upward inflection as if he's asking a question. Then, without moving his head off Pam, his eyes suddenly shift over to me. His glare strikes me, equivalent to a shock. My heart pounds. I feel the heat.

There is a long, unusual pause. It's the slice of space and time, an adjustment between opposite sexes. Boys, "men," can't help it. Their brains are relooping from fucking around to actually fucking. You can see it if you catch the pause. If you watch closely, the slight squirming. Their overheated, sweaty balls in need of rearrangement. The intrusion of new thoughts glazed with testosterone. Here they come. Who will be first? Here it is, the icebreaker!

"Who's your friend?" Scott asks.

Pam turns and looks at me. I am standing about six feet back. She throws a hitchhiker's thumb my way, smirking in wonder at what the hell Scott was asking.

"Who . . . her?" Pam asks, bewildered. "You know who she is, Scott. Don't be dumb."

"I think . . . uh . . . Grac . . . ?" he tries to muster.

"Don't start thinking Scott, you ass-wipe, might be dangerous!" Pam says, holding her hand up flat as a crossing guard would to keep traffic stopped, signaling to keep still and say nothing.

"Sheesh. Idiot. It's Mar—" Pam says, giving him a break.

"Ah, yeah, right. Marilyn's sister." Scott interrupts Pam, catching himself thinking out loud, slinking a bit in embarrassment of being "less than," at one time, to the hottest girl in high school.

"Yeah, ha, you've been there," Pam slips in, her snide remark sending the pent-up backseat boys into an outburst of whoops and hollers.

"Righhht," Scott says, resigning himself to the half-baked memory of a time not so great. Marilyn was a lot. His defeated tone indicates he couldn't please her. No one could. No one can and I wasn't going to let him in on that. As we "pussies" have few weapons in our arsenal, we have to guard each other's power.

"Idiots," Pam says while brushing the grass from her hands.

I catch Scott glance my way again, insecure. I find it amusing that he still didn't get my full name out. I am always the little sister. At this juncture, it doesn't matter. As usual, it is the Pam

Show now.

"Johnny's gonna love . . ." Pam continues, a pitch higher, close to yelling.

"Alright Pammy," Dean cuts in, impatient, bored, "let's make this right. Can we take you ladies somewhere?"

"We're waiting for friends," Pam says.

"Okay then, you need a smoke? A toke? What's your pleasure?" Dean says, whispering seductively, rattling off his wares.

Pam stares at the ground, thinking. A genuine and thoughtful moment.

"What about you two, maybe a few other friends too, if you want, come to Tony's party Friday night?" Scott breaks in. Idiot #2 hems, protesting from the backseat, but Dean glares at him in the rearview mirror. He bows his head and settles reverently.

"That'll work," Pam declares. "We want carte blanche with the party offerings." She turns and looks at me, "Whattaya want to drink?" Par for the course, as usual, without waiting for my answer, she turns around and says, "A fifth of Seagrams and a six-pack—make that a twelve-pack of Molson. Golden. Si. Vous. Plait."

"Ehhh, y-y-ou got it," Scott replies. He turns to Dean who gives a nod. "We'll see you ladies later then."

Ladies?

Scott hits the side of the door twice with his hand, a "giddy up" to Dean, who takes two fingers to his forehead, offering a loose, military-like wave as they peel off, screeching louder than when they came, reinforcing the skid marks, which serve as neighborhood reminders of who rules the roost.

"Cool, right?" Pam turns to me, smiling, eyebrows up as if she just bagged a cat.

"Totally," I reply, enthused in agreement, but I wiggle a little, physically in discomfort due to having peed my pants.

The clunker speeds off. Next stop, to the house of the guy we get pot from sometimes, to catch a quick hit before school. He recently bought this new electronic or mechanical bong—something new and enhanced in the world of "bongography."

The buzz from the shot of whiskey Pam and I downed before we left my house has been scared away by the wanna-be outlaws. We wait for a few more of our friends, moving in slow circles around each other, touching each other's shoulders, and running our hands down each other's arms. A little dance, weaves in with a little bored, waiting, as if nothing happened. Nothing really to talk about at that age (fifteen) in those times (the seventies). Everything is as it is supposed to be. Anything that is not will soon settle to that next level of midwestern-bred malaise, carried in the air and spread like pixie dust. It keeps everyone moving along in life.

2

PARTIES. HIGH SCHOOL. They play out like movie scenes. Best described in film editing terms: establishing shot, fade in, fade out, jump cut, hard cut, the montage, wipe, dissolve, rack focus, span, swish pan, Dutch angle, aerial, eye-level, extreme close up, and extreme long shot. Thanks to Pam and her demands after the showdown, we arrive, excited, ready and willing.

"Check out this house!" Pam says in awe as we approach the very large front door. There is a giant knocker in the shape of a lion's head, its wide-open mouth serving as the actual knocker. *Fitting. Walking into the lion's den no doubt. Raw meat.*

"I knew Tony was rich but really, when have I been on this side of town? I had no idea Tony was rich . . . like this," Pam says as she starts banging the knocker firmly, more than once. I don't feel the need to tell her who Tony "Jr."'s father is. She'll figure it out soon enough. After all, Pam's dad is the local vet;

with the crematorium in their basement and the pet cemetery in her backyard, her dad has to know Tony "Jack" Sr.

A very thin, tiny woman, wearing a sheer black dress, silky black hair pulled back tight in a bun, sculpted cheekbones, and a pointy dancer's nose angled upward, answers the door, greeting us with a big toothy smile. Her gold jewelry drips, chains, varying in width, encasing her body—from ears to chest, to waist, to shoes. If piled onto a scale, the mass would surely outweigh her body.

"Ah . . . young ladies!" she softly sings. "Lovely to have you in our home. This way, this way."

Before she can take us all the way through the grand marble foyer decorated with paintings depicting violent biblical themes, the lion knocker hits again, so she waves us along toward the basement door and sashays to welcome the next group of arrivals.

"Ah . . . oh . . . it's you." I can hear her tone change to a light snarl. "Why aren't you using the back door, as usual?" With a literal hop, skip, and jump, Dean is right behind us on the basement stairs heading down to the game room.

"Pammmmmy!" he shouts.

"Deeeean!" she coos her best coo (not easy for Pam).

They exchange greetings as old friends would, in fact maybe even more so, and I wonder where I had been the past week that they might have graduated to this kind of somewhat intimate rapport. I shoot Pam a look. She shrugs and accepts his hand, and the two of them dance into the party. I stop at the bottom of the steps to take it all in.

Fade in: The first thing I note is Tony's black eye.

Fade out.

Fade in: Groups of two or three gathered around the room. A few playing pool. Many by the bar.

A jump cut to the fourteen-carat gold sink.

Fade out.

Fade in to Tony approaching me. Always polite, always a gentleman.

"Grace! I'm so glad you're here. Nice to see you," he says as he reaches out both arms, lunging in to kiss me on both cheeks. He is a little too syrupy for my taste but he is consistently nice, and for his purposes and placement in life, authentically so. I am one of the "little" people. I bring no harm. I am female. I am to be protected. Kept. Nice. Pretty. Vulnerable.

Hard cut to my face, confused as to why he has such a shiner glowing from his left eye.

"Why?" I say, gesturing with my finger to his eye

"Yeah, my father's a lefty," he replies with a half-hearted laugh.

"Oh, I, um . . . ha, right!" I trip on my words, baffled. I had been inquiring about *the* black eye, not which eye, but I catch his drift. I am intrigued but not surprised by his retort. While some fathers' souls are reinforced with shards of steel, all of our fathers, in this era, are cut from the same cloth—tough guys.

"I, yeah, um, why?" I ask, with partial focus on wanting to understand but also already retired to accept the status quo— that we all got the back of the hand or the belt at one time or another.

"Yeah, I pissed him off. It's okay. It happens. Toughens me up."

"Of course," I reply. I am skeptical but, yet again, not surprised. Later, I find out Tony Sr. was not happy Tony Jr. lost a game of pool to a girl the night before. That was it. An argument ensued. Jr. talked back to Sr., disrespecting him, and the ol' lefty threw one to Jr.'s right.

Tony lets one hand drop, ever so gently. I note his very soft hands, with polished nails. In turn, I note my nails are not polished but cracked and bitten, including the cuticles, and my skin rough from not enough self-care.

He pulls me into the party. I didn't think I'd get such a gracious debut. It all felt so . . . so natural . . . for him.

"Let's get you a drink," he says. "What will you be having?"

"I, um, sure," I bumble. "Whatever you have in mind . . . to make me. Whatever you have."

Close up: gold sink.

Tony excuses himself, observing something across the room to tend. *Wipe.*

The scene unfolds in front of me. A joint comes my way but I pass it along. I walk over to the wall of sliding glass doors to the outdoor pool area, cutting through those who plant themselves in cozy collectives of low, sunken chaises and pillowed nooks. I notice small smeared mirrors on various tables along the way.

Montage.

Music. Smoke—lots of it, both cigarettes and pot.

I sit on the side of the pool, kick off my flip-flops, hike up my skirt and put my feet in the water. Tony beelines for me and hands me my drink.

"Old Fashioned," he says proudly. It has an orange slice and a cherry skewered by a decorative umbrella leaning over the rim.

"Oh, wow, thanks," I say. Not the usual whisky shots and Red Cup keggers.

"My pleasure. I'll check you in a bit," he says, and off he wanders, from guest to guest—some fish-out-of-water, some spoiled, some stoned—to catch ashes from cigarettes and slip coasters under the drinks.

The next thing I feel is something of great mass grazing above me. There is a brief breeze atop my feathered blonde head. A heavy presence, in mid-air, right up and over me, curled to cannonball.

SPLASH!

Dean, fully clothed, sends water in all directions, unleashing a barrage of followers. One girl there, who loves to cause trouble, always upping the ante (I think her name is Barbie), is next. She probably dared Dean to do this. She's that kind of fun-bad-good-girl. The queen bee of her grade, who parties hardy with stoners even though she's with that hunk from the football team, Mike. Prom royalty. The three of them tag-team, really working people up to jump in. And they do. More than twenty people, fully clothed, drinks in hand, all in various positions, launch. Hurling at reckless speeds, displacing pool water with their masses, they splash like space capsules to great cheers from those too timid or smart to follow.

I see Pam right there, next to Dean. I thought Dean would be pissed at her clinging to him, but attaching to Pam could lead to being anointed into her brother Johnny's circle. Social climbing is not only for the rich and famous. Everyone has circles they want to penetrate.

To no avail, Tony shouts at everyone to get out of the pool. He tries to block the next wave of jocks, stoners and geeks, who take flying leaps over the heads of those already in the pool.

"Hey guys . . . uh . . . ah . . . shit!" Tony throws his hands in the air, waving. "What the hell, assholes! Assholes!"

No one is listening. One after another, they jump. Some are so stoned that they form single-file, zombie-like, and take the pool steps. Tony keeps trying to coax those in, out. Everyone continues to ignore him, screaming with delight and terror, plastered and whooping it up. I can see Tony is becoming more and more flustered. I back up and away, not wanting to get wet, nor be wet, from the spray extending far beyond the perimeter of the pool. I grab a lounge chair and slip into it to observe the chaos. There is a flash of light above and behind me. I look back and up. Tony's mom peers out the window.

"Hey, put your drink down. Come on," is a whisper in my ear. I turn my head back around to see Scott. I do not know where he had been or even if he had been here at all during the evening. He came out of nowhere.

"Why?" I inquire.

"Just come. Now," he replies, more of an order, with a look on his face that projects more concern than mischief or even romance. We head around the side of the house; Scott grabs my hand, not as an amorous gesture, but more so to hurry me along, to get to the front of the house, and out to the street.

"My car's down—," Scott says when he is cut short by a loud CRACK! coming from the back of the house.

CRACK!

CRACK!

Screaming. Yelling.

Kids, sopping wet, their belongings in hand, run out front now too, from both sides of the house, hauling ass to their cars, high-tailing it out of there.

"Tony's dad," Scott murmurs.

"He—"

"He knows how to clear the pool." Pause. "A twenty-two."

"Right," I say.

"Tony will have another shiner to match tomorrow," Scott says with a smirk. His laissez-faire attitude is both discomforting and intriguing.

At this moment I realize I'm becoming ordained into Scott's world. A sudden feeling of elevation registers, even though no one else is around to witness it. Suddenly I am protected. This night marks the first night of "us." Forever "us."

3

"THAT WAS CRAZY," I say to Scott.

"Yeah," Scott replies, in a volume indicating answering, more so, to himself. I can tell he is thinking about something else.

"How'd you know he was going to shoot off that gun?" I ask, interrupting his deep state. I worry for a minute that he might consider it a dumb question considering our community, our circles. Everyone has guns. Everyone around here hunts or thinks they have reasons to carry. I'm not crazy or blind. I can't think of a single friend whose father, brother or even mother for that matter, doesn't carry. But when it comes out at a kids' party? Not so cool.

No one will even question Tony Sr. Parents might chatter amongst themselves, declaring the action pompous, brazen, even stupid. Those who are card-carrying NRA members, who stack

The American Hunter magazines next to their La-Z-Boys, wear their reverence to responsible gun ownership as a badge of honor. Great pride drapes their silent stances. Those who don't toe the line mess it up for all, drawing attention to what the media chomp on to stir the pot, an often misinterpreted or misunderstood agenda. No, the parents won't be laughing Tony Sr. off. They are going to be pissed, watching closely, to figure out how to rechannel anything that might come of it. Of course, and in most cases, nothing ever does and life goes on as usual in this small bedroom community an hour west and a tad south of the Windy City.

"That's just Tony Sr.," Scott says, bringing his mind front and center again. "It's fucked up."

Not really the answer I am looking for, but I also don't know what I expect.

"Maybe take me to Pam's?" I pipe in to change the subject since it was all I was going to get from Scott on the matter. "I'm supposed to be sleeping over there."

"She's probably with Dean," Scott murmurs.

"Yeah, probably. I can wait on her porch or slip in her back door. They leave it open. Her parents sleep soundly, like rocks, dead to the world. They're on the far end of the house, the opposite side of that door. They never wake up. Ever."

"Hmmm." A man of few words for sure, I am learning. He continues, "I can wait with you in the car; we can hang out and listen to the radio."

I nod, shrug, "Sure."

Scott takes his eyes off the road and looks my way, raising an eyebrow at the thought of a possible make-out session. I hide a smile.

Waiting out front at Pam's, I notice the house lights are off. This is a signal to anyone coming home at this hour—they had better move like mice or fear the wrath of Pam's dad. He needs his eight hours so he can figure out what is wrong with all the animals, including farm animals, in and of the neighborhood. He's the hero of the community, the animal whisperer, able to understand the language of how the furry friends communicate their ills.

While we are waiting, Scott leans over and puts his arm around me. He pulls me close. It's nice, feels good, but it's a bit awkward. I remember my sister Marilyn probably planted her head on him the same way last year. I push that thought away. Marilyn has the attention span of a gnat, and as I am catching Scott's vibe more and more, she would have never had the patience for his slow-roll pacing. I give in and slouch into his hold, nuzzle in under his arm and slide my head upon his chest. I am surprised to hear his heart is not increasing in beats (whereas mine is about to jump out of my chest).

As soon as I start to relax, we hear tires screeching, a loud engine roaring up from behind us. Pam's brother Johnny comes hauling up the driveway in his tricked-out truck. Flinging the door open, he leaps out and lunges toward the garage, pulling brusquely on the handle to open it. Off Johnny's force, the garage door flies up into the rafters, shaking and rattling its nuts-to-bolts housing before settling. The garage light turns on automatically, set at a severe wattage to scare the hell out of intruders. Johnny freezes for a minute, having discovered something in the picture that is not usually there: us. With a mass of one of those barbaric cartoon monsters, he robotically pivots around and stares us down. Scott comes to attention and sits up straighter. Clears his throat.

Johnny struts down the driveway toward our car. Before he can reach us, Scott pushes the door open and hops out.

As they meet up, another car creeps up the road assessing to stop or, if trouble, pass by, perhaps even turn around. They pull up and I realize it's Pam and Dean.

"You . . ." Johnny points to me.

"Grace," Scott says.

"I got it," Johnny barks back. "You and . . . where is that firecracker sister of mine?" he scoffs. "Pam, fucking A," he says, shaking his head when he sees her with Dean.

Pam is getting out of the passenger side of Dean's old brown 'burnished saddle' Buick Electra.

"What? What?" she says in a snarking manner but it is rhetorical. She's seen this act before.

"Come on Grace," she orders me. "We gotta go inside."

"Go in the house," Johnny orders, even though he hears what Pam said. "Your night is over."

Pam rolls her eyes.

Scott shoots me a look, unrequited love, interrupted romance. I can feel his heartstrings pulling on mine. I want to stop and turn around and run to hug and kiss him, really kiss him, but Pam is pulling my arm, tugging me toward the house. Scott is walking backward to make sure he keeps his eyes locked on mine. Eventually his attention cedes to Johnny.

"You two . . . " Johnny says looking at Scott and then Dean, as he walks back up to the garage, "Your nights are just beginning."

Johnny stomps right to the workbench, picks up a wrench, and throws it to Dean, who catches it with ease, swinging it back to mellow the ferociousness of its flight speed. With the same velocity comes the bully club directly at Scott, who catches it with the same finesse as Dean. Johnny then grabs a wooden baseball bat, holding it at the top, his large hand wrapped around it tight, arms tense, muscles at attention for action.

He grabs the rope of the garage door to yank it back down; it reverberates from the force, banging to the ground. We hear this from the front porch as we stop to watch the boys before heading inside the house. I wonder if Pam's dad is going to wake up. If he does, would he want the downlow to what's going on?

My parents feign "not hearing a thing" to avoid any drama; it is easier for them to bury their heads in the sand.

Johnny slaps the fat end of the bat into the palm of his other hand which makes a loud, deep slapping—

THWAP.

"That's the sound of a kneecap getting crushed," Johnny says to no one and everyone. "Let's go."

No one asks where. They hop into Johnny's crew cab Chevy. The truck backs up into the street and comes to a complete stop. The chicken lights ignite. They peel down the road, burning rubber. They're not going after chicken thieves.

4

"EENY, MEENY, MINY, moe. Catch a tiger by the toe. If he hollers, let him go, eeny, meeny, miny, moe," Pam and I recite in unison under the covers of her floral canopy bed, perched with pillows, taking turns holding the Ace Hardware utility flashlight to see what fate has in store for each of us. We add a phrase or two to change the outcomes if we don't get what we want.

"My mother told me to pick the very best one, and Y-O-U are not it!" Pam. "He-he."

"Y-O-U, I said, Y-O-U are not it, it, it!" I take it further when it's my turn, snapping the paper together harder near the end of the saying before the corner is turned up to reveal my destiny.

We had made that four-square, "Fortune Teller," origami game from a scrap piece of paper. On the inside are eight flaps, each concealing the choices we chose to determine our futures:

four guys, four houses, four places in the world, and four numbers representing our offspring.

We play and manipulate them to land on Scott for me and Dean for her, but change up where, what we'll call home and how many rugrats will be running around.

"Dean. Chicago. A house. Two kids."

"Bob . . . no Scott, Scott. Cabin. California."

"D-D-Dean. Canada. Fishing cottage. Four kids."

"S-S-S-S-Scott. New York City. House. One kid. Naw that won't do. I wanna have a lot of his babies."

"Ha! Hawaii, four kids, a farm and yeah, Dean," Pam laughs. "Hawaii! I'll learn how to surf."

"Why do you pick such unrealistic places? You're not going to Hawaii," I reply. "Dean will burn. Ghost boy. Pale face."

"Way to burst my bubble," Pam sneers at me. "As if New York City is more realistic for you? And Scott? You think he's gonna leave that mother-fucking crazy family of his? That prince? His mother still has her umbilical cord attached to him."

"Ha, yeah. She's crawled so far up his ass, it's beyond," I reply. "But I'm going to make movies or TV shows or something. I'm getting outta here, that's for sure. I'm gonna write about you assholes. You'll be a TV show. A soap opera. *One Life to Live.*"

"Whatta'll be the name?" Pam giggles. "*'One Life to Ruin? Drugs, Sex and Rock and Roll . . . Due to Boredom?'* Or, a game show, *'Who's the Dick?'* Or, *'What'd Tony Junior Do Now to Get Another Black Eye?'*"

"Ha, yeah, with . . . prizes! Behind door one you get a baseball bat to beat on people, and door number two you get free gas for a year to go cruising—" I add in.

"Yeah, especially in Dean's boat-of-a-car! We need that," Pam interupts.

"Or the curtain where Carol Merrill is standing, you get a

ticket outta here!" I say.

"You wish," Pam replies haughtily.

"I do."

"Maybe my dad's vet business can be a show."

"Ha, ha, ha, with the crematorium."

"Like whose dog is that smell?" Pam laughs.

"Arrgrrrrfff, gross!"

"I'mma gonna . . .," Pam screams while laughing louder, "oh my God, I can't hold it any longer! Right? Totally prime. Choice. For sure."

"Come here," I say as I grab Pam around the neck and pull her close.

"What, what . . . ah, okay," says Pam. "My hair . . . ouch, my hair."

I can't help but hold her for a minute longer. Her smell. Her warmth. We are more than friends; sisters perhaps.

"Come on. Let's do pinky, pinky swear, blood sister, together forever, 'til death do us part, 'til the end!" I chant.

"Til the end. The very end. The very fucking-A end!" Pam says as she extends her hand to me. I grab my mini-switchblade and I jab the pad on her pinky finger. She doesn't wince. Then I stab mine. It's much easier to do to myself. I feel nothing. We twist our pinkies around the other's and then make sure each drop of blood matches up and is mixed.

"Til the end!" We say in unison, locking eyes.

5

"YOU DO THE toast," Pam waves me to the other side of the kitchen. I'm still surveying the adjoining family room where Scott and Dean are asleep on an L-shaped couch. Their heads are close, almost touching.

"Pam, look!" I say pointing to them. I'm surprised to find them there. I give Pam a sideways glance.

"I'm sure Johnny told them to crash here," Pam answers as she starts to pull pans out of the cupboards and the eggs, butter, jam, bologna, ketchup, mustard, mayo, and hot sauce from the fridge.

"They're charming when unconscious," I say.

"Awww. Tweedle Dee and Tweedle Dum!"

"You're so mean!"

"Am not. It's true. They're numbskulls," Pam laughs.

"I think they're cuuuute," I purr.

Pam's dad enters the kitchen. He surveys the counter—eggs, sliced bologna, the large skillet, all the condiments. He nods approvingly.

"The usual Pammy, my sweetie?" he growls softly.

"Sure thing Daddy," she replies. I'm amazed she still calls him that. They are either syrupy-sweet in their love for each other or he's throwing her out of the house, followed by her shoes, one at a time, aimed for her head. She never fails to turn and flip the bird, while catching them. Love, hate, hate, love.

"Make sure you make me a plate. Add some chips on the side. Make mine before those two knuckleheads smell the fried bologna and crawl their silly asses over here," he says.

"Yup. You got it—" says Pam.

"Daaadddddy," I chime in.

Pam snorts and starts greasing up a pan.

I'm surprised her dad is not surprised to see Dean and Scott on the couches. He must have known what was going on.

John Sr. turns to me and raises one very hairy eyebrow. "Don't you ever go home?"

"My parents are away—," I reply, and then whisper, ". . . again."

"You're always here when they're not away too," Senior mumbles. He looks me over, up and down. He tilts his head to crack his neck and turns to face the boys, still sleeping. Dean's mouth is open. Scott is curled in a ball, no blanket. Dean has both blankets.

Senior shakes his head. "Yeah, your parents, I saw them the other day. They look like movie stars," he says to me, while he continues staring at the boys.

"Hmmm," I reply out of courtesy. I don't really like to talk about my parents or hear what others think of them.

"They are climbing that ladder, huh?"

"I guess, I don't know," I reply.

"Humprfff, yeah, they are," says Senior.

The eggs and bologna splatter in the butter, crackling. A loud snap. It happens when the bologna makes a little heat bubble and then implodes on itself. This wakes both Scott and Dean, who open their eyes but don't move. They are surveying the room. They spy Pam's dad. Dean rolls his eyes back and closes them again. He picks up on that he is in for some kind of scrutiny. We call it "the treatment."

Scott looks my way. I'm pleased with this. It's a sweet moment, soon to be interrupted by Senior.

"I am assuming that everyone slept in their respective places. Pammy?" Senior says, no longer mumbling.

"Yes, Daddy," Pam replies as she flips the eggs and the now-burnt bologna. She tosses grated cheese on top of the spread and covers the pan, then turns to lean against the counter, looking directly at her dad. He clocks her to make sure she is not lying. Pam is known to lie. She's a liar when she needs to be. He stares at her for a long minute. Then he turns to the boys on the couch.

"Look at you two," he laughs. "Pansies, huh?"

Dean and Scott don't dare answer. They've learned, as we've all learned, there is no right answer. I'm assuming he's making fun of them because neither of them made a move on either of us last night. Not man enough to do so under his roof. And if they did, and they hemmed and hawed about not being pansies, they'd be getting their asses thrown out pronto. No "Pammy" breakfast for them. So they take the Alpha-elder male abuse. Scott looks to Dean for any kind of response, any silently-coded guidance. Afterall, it is his girl's house. Her dad. Dean shrugs and twitches his head to a tilt, with a grimace, imparting nonverbally to Scott that it's par for the course.

"But you'll make a ruckus in the neighborhood," Senior continues to bait the boys, "won't you?"

"Here Daddy, take your plate on the patio," Pam says as she scoops a heap of 'heart-attack heaven' onto a large plate. She moves quickly, getting her dad out of the kitchen and away from Dean and Scott before anyone slips up.

"Grace! Where's the toast!" Pam shouts.

"Shit!" I reply, remembering I have eight pieces in the two toasters. They popped a beat ago.

"What are ya good for if you can't even make toast, Gracie?" Senior snorts, grabbing his plate and two pieces of toast. He makes off with the butter, soft and ready to be spread, in the ceramic cow butter dish. Pam rolls a fork and knife in a paper towel and slips it into her dad's back pocket. His pants hang real low on his flat, wide butt, which is disproportionately, and in no way, balanced by the island-unto-itself mass of a stomach protruding on his other side. Without warrant or reason, this God-given shape holds up his six-foot-four, 240-pound frame.

The boys breathe a sigh of relief that Senior's attention on them has waned. They sit up, cautious. Dean looks to Pam with puppy eyes for permission to approach. She nods and smiles. It is then I am sure, at some quiet minute of the night, she did leave me in that princess bed for his arms. I'm not sure when or where but I know. I can tell. As Pam passes me to greet Dean I whisper "slut" in her ear. She grins on her way by, confirming her dalliance.

The four of us sit at the kitchen table. Scott and Dean wolf down their food. They seem naively astounded when Pam offers them seconds. I pick at my plate, feeling awkward about eating in front of Scott. Scott notices this and makes a movement with his fork and eggs, insinuating that I should do the same. *All* I can do is stare at his lips. They are perfect squiggles, and pale rose in color. His shaggy, dirty-blonde, sand-colored hair hangs in his bluer-than-blue eyes, his eye-lashes thick, like awnings over windows. Is he really becoming mine?

"So who took it last night?" Pam asks about their bat, wrench, and billy club operation.

Dean gives Scott a look and they both remain silent.

"Oh come on!" Pam proclaims. "I can just ask Johnny later."

Senior walks back into the room. "Who took what?"

"Nothing," says Pam.

"Nothing is always something," her dad scoffs and piles another helping on his plate.

"You want more toast?" I ask, trying to make up for my past faux pas.

"Oh, now you're stepping up? Too late," her dad says as he exhales as if even speaking was exasperating to him. "I'll tell you what, Gracie, you can come sweep the ashes out of the burner later, huh?"

"Daddy!" Pam screams. "Grace is not going to do that."

"Geez, whattabout these two dingbats?" nodding to Scott and Dean.

"Um, yes sir, sure," Dean replies.

"Uh, sure. Sir," Scott adds, mimicking Dean.

Senior gives a small smile and turns back to the patio.

Dean and Scott look at each other and laugh, which makes us all break out in laughter.

"What's so funny-ee?" Pam's mom, Polly, interrupts as she enters the kitchen. Her voice is melodic, always ending on an 'up' inflection from ingrained Celtic roots.

"Nothin'," Pam.

"Nothing is . . ."

"Always something," we all contribute, but not at the same time, imitating Pam's dad.

"So, Johnny was here, huh," Polly states more than asks.

"Um . . . when do you mean?" asks Pam.

"Don't mess with me Pamela."

"Pammmm-ee-laaa!" we all repeat in squeals, laughing.

"He was going after that boy that disrespected your sister," Polly says flippantly while seeking her favorite coffee mug. When she discovers Scott has it, she grabs another, a Rudolf mug. She walks over to Scott, pours his coffee in the Christmas mug and returns with her mug in hand to pour herself some coffee. She doesn't bother rinsing it.

"Yup. You don't mess with my chickens. That's a fact," Polly says. She raises her mug, in a toast, mostly to herself, that this household, this hen house, while roosters abound, is run by this hen, without an ounce of doubt.

6

POT.

OLD MILWAUKEE.

Speed.

20 gauge.

Sex.

Jack and Coke.

Strawberry double-dose T (swallow one and gum the other).

12 gauge (longer range a bit older but more kick—mostly for ducks and geese).

Roar 714s (a.k.a. lemmons).

Hash.

9-mm Glock 16.

A little more sex.

Mesc(aline).

12-gauge scope with a slug barrel.

Chasing the dragon.

Speed.

270 rifle.

More sex.

More pot.

347 scope for hunting (big handgun)

Southern Comfort and OJ.

Blotter acid (dots of Disney characters—I choose Mini).

38 Special.

Hash (under a glass).

Sex here (Dean liked it when Pam packed her small revolver in her bra—loaded, no doubt).

Kamikazes.

Smith & Wesson 9mm (doesn't kick as much as a 40 caliber).

Pot.

A 44 (will stop anything in its tracks)

Molsen Golden.

6 Hauser (hard to control to reshoot).

LSD.

556 80-round (good for target shooting because they don't kick).

More pot.

White Russians.

And sex there. And there and there. And there.

We measure our summers, every summer, by the smell of the breeze, which comes and goes, in gentle cascades across Lake Huron; in the beer we drink, the drugs we do, the love we make, the guns we shoot and the bullets that fly, making a sound, slicing that warm, balmy air, after the bang. Year after year. Years since Tony Jr.'s party. We were all coming up on college or no college and trade jobs or going into family business, large and small. Our good times together, of our youth, build like a wave coming up behind us, to slowly but surely, push us into our futures, willingly or not.

But not yet. We hang on, like a string to a balloon, to every summer by that lake.

Thanks to Scott and his family, every other weekend we road trip up to his hunting cabin, across M46, south of Saginaw Bay on the east side of the state of Michigan. Long summer days of drinking, smoking, tripping and shooting at cans, bottles, and small animals when the spirit moves us; making the four of us inseparable. We have a bond so strong, the four of us, that Scott and I would feel incomplete without Pam and Dean. My relation to Scott is reliant on my relation to Pam and to Dean. It is certainly not unusual to any of us, but I suppose someone on the outside looking in might consider it too close, bordering on codependency. We were four peas in a pod and we saw no reason to not ever be together, now and forever. The future was ours to keep.

Scott's family was originally a bird hunting family. Most of the guns had no real value. Mostly sentimental.

"You got them however you got them. They start to, well . . . pile up," Scott explains. Shotguns to rifles for deer hunting, a few bows to play the winds, a real sport.

Scott's crazy uncles visit a day here, a day there, excited for what they call "shotgun zone." They have a muzzle loader single shot. Uses a 50-caliber bullet. Or the Flint Log 1750s with two little powder chargers, pack the ball in.

"Now they have powder cartridges! Fifty grams of powder with powder charges, a ramrod, a shotgun shell primer," one Uncle screams with joy, "It's a right shot and a clean kill."

Another Uncle talks endlessly about "exchangeable barrels, over-under, top and bottom—double barrels. Slugs out of one and shotgun shells out of the other. Screw things on the end of it, different chokes, wider spread."

Slapping knees, sharing stories: one about the time Scott took his dad to the doctor and the receptionist asked for his insurance card and his dad accidentally pulled his gun from his belt and placed it on the counter. Apparently, without missing a beat, she said to him, "Well Senior, you make sure that chamber ain't full and put that pretty little girl back at 4:00 p.m. We won't be checking that today. I need you to get me the more important proof of your manhood—that you can pay!"

Scott likes all the guns but he doesn't obsess about them. He is most fond of his 12-gauge shotgun—a Sears and Roebuck from the 1930s. It was a Browning with a big drop where the thumb goes, with a recoil pad where the rubber hardened up— so not really having a recoil pad at all. He grew up shooting it.

Scott's uncle also built him an AR-15. He keeps it in the corner of his designated room at the cabin. It has a Mini-30 with a magazine—semi-automatic—but it's not a machine gun. There are waterbeds, one in his room and one other room, at the cabin. Not so much for "the motion of the ocean"—more so for protection. If anyone comes in shooting, the water in the bed deflects the bullets from this initial shoot out before anyone skilled in the fine art of militia procedures has to grab any one of the AR-15s stationed in each corner of those rooms.

Scott starts every session with all the guns lined up behind us. In advance of us joining, he walked off the distance to the target marking feet with old rope and large sticks. Pam is super badass with that AR-15 with the flip-up site. From a hundred yards, she nails her rounds within inches of the bullseye. I love the Smith & Wesson. It had an easy slide, unlike the Glock, and a dual pistol grip safety.

Regardless of the gun, Scott wraps his body around mine,

holding his hands around my hands, his chin on my shoulder, his breath on my neck. The warmth of his front side to my back side generates a heat between our bodies, electricity, an intense magnetic field. When we pull the trigger together, the kick throws me back into him. He holds strong and firm.

***

I have never felt more protected, more loved, more secure than when I'm with Scott, at his cabin, shooting. Lightness of being, a sense of calm. Everything is alright in the world. And we measured another summer.

7

"THERE IS NO sense in pretending. Your eyes give you away. Something inside you is feeling like I do. We said all there is to say," we belt out, top of our lungs, really loud, really bad, on our way to this tiny little dive in Chicago's Old Town. Because the day is beautiful, the kind of beauty that makes one mindless, feeling like floating on air, we get lost on side roads detouring into and through the South Side to take in its colorful and soulful, if not slightly precarious, ambiance. It is the kind of neighborhood where you keep the windows down and music blaring to display your sense of assumed connection with *that* community, but the click of the auto-lock on the doors keeps that link in its proper place in reality. Autumn brings with it a crispness to promote bulky sweaters, jean jackets and weathered leather boots.

"Baby Breakdown, go ahead and give it to me. Breakdown honey take me through the night. Breakdown now I'm standing here can't you see. Breakdown, it's alrightttttttt. It's alrighttttt. It's al—"

CRUNCH!

Screeching and swerving. My head bobs, whiplashing, the force of no control. I hear Scott yell, "Ff-F-F-FUCK!"

"S-S-S-SCOTT!" I scream, not fully grasping whether this actually comes out of me or is in my head. My tongue is sticking to the back of my front teeth, my lips purse, glue together tight in fear.

Pam and Dean are in the back seat.

I never hear them scream.

8

CLICK-TICK. CLICK-TICK. CLICK-TICK.

I open one eye. I feel a coating on my face. A veil. A sheer curtain. It feels dusty, but thicker, small shavings of trimmed hair from a quick haircut. My clenched jaw allows only a sliver of my mouth open to exhale. I blow off the "hairs." It's a major effort for barely any breath. What I see hit the air is light and clear and in crystal form.

Glass.

I inhale through my nose, with care and caution, and exhale harder this time, pushing my lower lip further out to make sure my breath funnels right up over my face. Larger shards take flight and drop fast. My lap is covered in even bigger chunks of glass. My right eye does not open so I glance, carefully, with my left. I see Scott's head tilted back, bleeding at the forehead. I cannot turn my neck around to see Dean and Pam. I don't need to.

Pam is up on the side of the road. Her body contorted beyond any hope. Disjointed arms. Her leg wrapped behind her, backwards, with a foot twisted another ninety degrees further. Her face is one glassy sheet of fresh blood. She is scalped. Made of steel, never to be messed with, now all a facade, a betrayal beyond her body; one of her soul.

I do not see Dean.

Click-tick. Click-tick. Click-tick.

That sound. The turn signal is jammed.

The other car is tossed up onto its side, in the ditch that separates the road from the Jack-In-The-Box at that intersection.

I see three guys in that car and there is a fourth, outside the car, in a white shirt soaking quickly to red. Blood. Face planted, body bent, legs broken backwards. A smaller car than our Caddy, a beat up clunker, completely totaled.

Sirens, from afar, grow louder. In no time we are surrounded by three patrol cars, a fire engine, and last to arrive, two EMS trucks. Everyone gets to work quickly. Roping off the roads, diverting traffic, triaging the situation. I sit still, in silence. I let go. Of everything. I have to. I have to let go of everything. I need to breathe. I need to sleep. I need to let go. At the same time that I am relaxing, to let go, to let someone help me, I am remembering one thing. One important thing.

***

It is the first time I experience, "there is nothing we can do about it." And in truth, since "it" is every moment in life, I'm surprised we don't live like that all the time.

Pam died instantly.

Dean survived but lost a leg and suffered from severe, chronic back issues. He leaned heavily into relieving the pain before he overdosed five years to the day after the accident.

The police were "nice" enough, knowing Scott's father, who is a labor union negotiator, well known to the Chicago Boys in Blue. They disregarded the trunk full of guns and ammo, passing it off with a comment that we got lucky we were not hit from behind as it could have been "a real shit show," "explosion-city," "mother-fucking lights out."

The kid thrown from the other car died instantly. His body just as splayed out, damaged, twisted into deformity as Pam's and Dean's but mind was not paid to him. He would be inventoried later.

No witnesses. No other evidence. Those other three kids, from the South Side, just on the other side of what everyone referred to as "the boundary," the driver, will be tried for manslaughter, and later convicted. The two who survived will not have stories told about them. Border mishaps get buried due to the same conclusion for the 'others' all too often.

Scott saw the red light.

I saw the red light.

We both saw the red light. The only ones who saw it, too late. We never spoke of it, ever.

Click-tick.

PART II
Trials
New York City. 1990s

9

"CAN'T YOU GET her to *at least* argue with the puppy adopter? After all, she made this match. Shouldn't she *at least* go to the extreme measures that it is the correct match?" screams the Puppy Matchmaker reality show producer. I freeze. I'm numb. This half-my-age dip-shit is literally screaming at me, and my crew, but mostly at me, directly at my face, in my face, way too close. I did not cut my teeth in this industry for twenty-five plus years to suddenly find myself inches away from a crazed lunatic who thinks that *this* is the most important show on TV. *Reality show* on TV. I mean *really.* Really? There are so many more super important reality shows airing right now, and so many more super important reality stars. Kardashians rule the roost. Every housewife from any show everywhere now gets paid to show up at restaurants and nightclubs. The branding of *that* one who is super thin. The dating shows or marriage shows. Teen moms and moms with a record number of fetuses sharing a womb.

People who compete by eating worms or putting themselves in containers with poisonous insects. Fat Jersey kids who drink too much and swear a lot. These are America's crown jewels of reality, and I've got a pint-size producing bitch, with a paid-for-by-daddy media degree from some mediocre East Coast liberal arts school that only accepted her because mommy and daddy agreed to make hefty donations during her tenure there. This is *what* is yelling at me, inches away, so close that when she spits with any pronunciation of her "p's" or "st's," she nails me.

"I'm not sure we are getting our day's worth here with quality footage. Tell your crew we're working OT," she said in a tattle-tell voice.

"You're paying."

"What? What was that? Oh, if I am, it's coming out of the director's salary!"

"Can't do that."

"To hell I can't! I can DO whatever I want to DO."

I try to walk away. I do. She is following me, wagging her finger. I can see it from the corner of my eye. The crew is standing there waiting for mommy (that'd be me, their director) to give direction. Our "star" is stroking a freaked-out puppy, and the adopter is in shock, wondering what she has gotten herself into.

What is more humiliating is that my crew has to endure it too. They have to watch her continuously pulverize me verbally.

Realizing this, I snap.

I snap.

My mind synchronizes with my neck, which jerks mercilessly to one side, causing, literally, a snapping sound. My body follows.

SNAP!

I begin to lunge but hang on for one split second, because I do, for one split second, feel personally responsible for the bread and butter my crew needs to put on their tables every night, but I also know that Little Miss Dip Shit needs to keep the show in production. She, no doubt, is thinking she can do my job. It's not rocket science. I perhaps, make it look easy. I am lucky. I have great teams. We crank out award-winning films and shows, which has positioned me as one of those very versatile directors who can do it all, and do it all well. Maybe too well. Because right then and there, I give it all up.

Ergo I do it. Simply flat out do it. And I'm guessing that in hindsight, I'll be glad I do because it frees me. It frees me of the grind that has taken hold of this industry; a business of spewing out total crap and, or, large over-the-top, ball-busting action films for fourteen-year-old boys and men who act as if they are fourteen-year-old boys. It frees me of any expectation that I have to continue in this industry. It frees me of myself.

I break free.

Thanks to my dad, who boxed in the Navy and taught all his kids how to throw a left, and then a right, I raise my fist ready to deliver my first blow. I stop mid-air. I realize I can't do this. What has always been so natural to me suddenly makes my arm feel a hundred pounds. I slowly lower it. I can feel the crew watching. I am at odds with myself. I am confused. Little Miss Dip Shit crosses her arms, in daring defiance to me and she smirks. She smirks!

And so, I spit.

On her face.

Yes. I spit on her face.

"Arrrggrhhh-ahhhhhhhhh," she screams. "Ewwwww, it smells like vodka!"

"Vodka has no smell you little bitch," I reply in a neutral tone, neither admitting nor denying there was any vodka in my saliva, which there was by the way—a pint full before noon.

The whole scene, in my mind, moves, again, in slow motion. First my fist, from my left side, where my thumb had been hanging on my left pocket, up and out and then over and up, only to come down again. My confusion. My spitting. I'm not sure what gives me greater pleasure at that exact moment—the sound I make when I spit or the look on her face when she became aware she had been spat upon. Besides her face contorting in disgust, which broke from slow-mo to a jump-cut sequence, I was able to take in my peripheral vision the sheer and utter joy that emanated from my crews' faces. It was awesome.

I am a hero.

For a minute.

Then all hell breaks loose. The two top executive producers (there are five—take note—this is a red flag when all five are "working" EPs and not silent EPs as they should be—and were in the *old days*) head my way, walking briskly, fists clenched, looking very unhappy—but not for the reason one might think. They are not so necessarily pissed off because I have spit on their pint-sized ditz producer. Well, they are, but not because I had, in fact, spit on her. They are upset because there is one saying running through any EP's mind at one time, at all times—TIME IS MONEY and MONEY IS TIME. They are pissed because for the ten minutes it takes the little shit to get over her shock and eventually fire me, they are losing money. Time, not well spent.

***

Things went back to normal for the show. The crew continued to work, without me, and I walked away—free.

The show never hit the air, by the way, and all that time spent spending money to make the half-assed show never amounted to any money made on all that time spent—which made me realize at that moment that time is always and will always be more valuable than money.

10

FREE IS GOOD for about thirty days. After thirty days, free
becomes a prison. Not that I'm acquainted with prison, but it is
what I assume prison to be. When I am in this "prison," I start,
at first, to look for ways to entertain myself through the long
bouts of, what many told me, would be "valuable time."

"You'll see. This will be good for you."

"It's just what you need."

"Fuck them. It's all on them. You'll be fine. This will do you good."

"Ah, meant to be. Happened for a reason."

Everyone meant well, but I wasn't having it. I had put a
few feelers out in the industry, to see what was up, where, but it
doesn't matter anymore. The industry has changed. I am older,
still a woman—and we all know the stats of female directors—or
lack of stats. I also now have the reputation of being *that* crazy
director. Crazy, by the way, only works in favor of male direc-

tors. They are not labeled crazy when they have their outbursts. They miraculously are knighted "geniuses." Women who complain about the "geniuses" become "bitter bitches."

To those who know better—the people who actually work in the industry, the DPs, the sound people, line producers, PAs, I am now folklore. Respected. Admired. But to the suited Hollywood-king wannabe's, I am the plague. Not to be hired. Too risky, too emotional, too dangerous. I get a couple sympathetic offers of consideration, but I don't want to end up working on the schlock projects ponied up to me because no one else of any value is interested.

So to this end, I am done. My career, one of the only reasons I got out of bed for the past twenty-five years—done. Finished. I could have sucked it up, apologized, kissed the ass of some twenty-something great granddaughter of William B. Mayer, who thought, because of her name, it was in her blood to have to carry on the reins of the family (even though she'd be destined to blow it in more cases than not, it is statistically proven that the third generation and those thereafter lose the fortune, the family business or both). But I didn't. Having the thought in my head of "No, I'm not going to do it" never went away and suddenly I find myself obsessed with making up for lost time and figuring out what this "lost time" consists of. I can't think at home. I am going stir crazy there with the three girls and a distant husband who all need tending. I can no longer tend—both physically and mentally. Every chore, draining. Every question, irritating.

"Mom, where's my . . ."

"Honey, how about that . . ."

"Mom, what's up with the . . ."

"Honey, do you know where my [fill in the blank] is?"

"Mom, I can't find my [fill in the blank]!"

I remember the game Pam and I used to play, Fortune Teller: *Eeny, meeny, miny, moe. Catch a tiger by the toe. If he hollers, let him go, eeny, meeny, miny, moe. My mother told me to pick the very best one, and Y-O-U are not it! Y-O-U, I said, Y-O-U are not it, it, it! Scott. New York City. House. One kid. Naw that won't do. I wanna have a lot of his babies.*

Funny I always wanted a big family and I am no good for them now. I have to get out. I want to leave. I love them. Perhaps too much? Do I? Is this why I have so much trouble showing it? They are my everything. To have something that means that much, weighs that much, is too much for me. It is painful. I am pained. I am dead.

The only thing that makes perfect sense to me, besides my desire to keep increasing alcohol consumption due to boredom of course, is to get out and walk. Walk and walk and walk.

I devise a walking plan, a grid, a strategy for walking every block in our neighborhood a certain way—tipsy or not. With or without a bottle or flask. Particular stores and addresses become checkpoints and each block serves a purpose. I want to go as fast as I can to figure out what time I have lost. I am determined to find out how to get it back. This seems productive and focused. All the right intentions for a decent outcome—to get into something new, a new job, a new career, teach, go to nursing school, perhaps work for a nonnn-pproffffffff—

THWAP.

Like that.

Just like that.

THWAP.

JOLT.

SCRAP.

I fall. I go down hard. I topple. First, onto my right shoulder. Then with a fierce jolt, my face slams to the ground. The rest of my body follows, obedient, scrapping, splaying me across the gravel road, with surprisingly similar ease, soft butter spread on bread. The unfathomable speed with which my body propels out and then down, across the road. There isn't even time for disbelief that I am going down. I am there.

Two people drag me to the curb to avoid a fast-turning taxi ready to sandwich any part of my body between rubber and cement. They prop me up against a building next to a puddle of dog pee, icing on the "tragedy cake," which completely bums me out.

"You alright, l-l-lady?" one cautiously asks.

Lady?

I nod. They step backward, away from me slowly, unsure of whether to leave me or not. This is New York City. No one in this city that never sleeps is really out and about without a plan, some place to go, someone to meet, a time constraint—and I had put a five-minute damper in theirs. At about ten feet, they turn and make their break. I'm sure they are thinking it could have been worse. Taken longer.

I sit there wincing in pain. I refuse to cry. "No room for tears in production"—is the saying—and I attribute that saying to about every other facet of life too.

***

As it turns out, what there is room for, in production, and in life, is *painkillers.* A visit to urgent care provides my first entry into the world of Oxy. What a miracle drug! No more pain (in so many ways). A few refills along, I should've been on my way but oh, the thrill of that buzz. My mind wired and ready precisely so. I was one of the "lucky" ones, who really adapts well to being addicted to Oxy. Some kind of connection to possible ADD or ADHD enhanced the drug's efficacy (although, I was never formally diagnosed, as was par for the course growing up in the seventies and eighties—one simply had a lot of energy and listening was not a strong suit).

Once cut off from the urgent care doctor, I set out to find new doctors, general practitioners and specialists. I became an expert in presenting my varied ailments, connecting everything to a chronic pain in the lower back, shoulders and hips. Doctors, as perfect clean-shaven dealers, were all too happy to push their drug sales, to promote for the pimps of Pfizer, Johnson & Johnson, or Merck, just to secure a complimentary, all-inclusive Caribbean cruise. This was a breaking headline by the time I was in the thick of it, already down the rabbit hole, where it was obvious to see that the execs sitting in the C-suites of big pharma were the drug lords, the doctors, the dealers, the perk vendors, and the pimps and we were the addicts. We were the whores. All legitimate and thus legal.

After I made my way through the local medical network, I headed out to Brooklyn, Queens and Long Island. Then up to the Bronx and Westchester. A few times further up the Hudson with valid practitioners. Eventually, I had to find the shady medical circuit—stealing my friend's husband's script pad (short-lived, no charges pressed), raiding my friends' and relatives' medicine cabinets (becoming a super friend to those in need after surgeries and illnesses), and learning to trade up or down on the streets to get what I wanted. What I needed. What I now need.

To move me along or avoid any long-winded explanations or revved-up confrontations, friends handed me their barely touched prescriptions of every size, flavor, and strength. Dylan's Candy gone bad. Sometimes, all I had to do was ask.

When you hug or kiss a loved one, your pituitary gland releases oxytocin. It's called the "love hormone." At the point of orgasm, the brain releases massive amounts of oxytocin *and* dopamine, the "feel-good" neurotransmitter connected to the reward center.

OxyContin, or "Oxy," works the same magic, increasing dopamine levels. It has no preference for whom it charms. It knows no victim to what becomes a boundless love affair.

OxyContin is actually a derivative of oxycodone and not of

oxytocin. But it might as well be. Oxytocin is a hormone used to help start or continue labor and to control bleeding after delivery. Sometimes it is used to help milk secretion in breastfeeding. Oxytocin is also a controversial hormonal injection that is used widely in the dairy industry to beef up cows and enhance their milk, which is then devoured by humans, possibly leading to premature puberty in young girls. On the black market, there is concern that the misuse of this growth booster is reported among trafficked children, injected to actually accelerate puberty among girls.

Oxytocin is now being used to help addicts wean off opioids such as OxyContin. The correlation becomes obvious: plump, happy, horny and high.

Climbing up the next level of relief in the ladder of addiction. In its purest form, a perfect visualization of it. "Gateway to" is the capitalist's softened messaging. One cannot obstruct the inherent right to do business in this country: booze, cigarettes, saturated fats, sex and pills. A welcome mat, a door wide open, to never having to feel any pain. Ever.

I am a long way from sipping mommy's drinks as a child. A child who loved to spin around and get dizzy enough to fall down. A child who chose to hyperventilate as a way of changing up the status quo, squelching the boredom or baiting to switch the flight or fight chaos in her household. A child who learned to self-medicate with alcohol and soft drugs as an accepted form of recreation, no more and no less. I am a long way away from her.

I am in heaven.

11

"BEEP. BEEP. BEEP."

Again.

"Beep. Beep. Beep."

The clock by Chloe's bed beeps loudly; 5:30 a.m. She wakes early to get a jump on things. I faintly hear her. I'm familiar with this routine. The oldest of three. Sixteen. Similar to many her age, she is obsessed with learning how to drive, but for Chloe her reason is stealth, almost life or death: to get the hell out of this apartment, away from her parents, her siblings, this city, drive fast and far, and never look back. Certainly now more than ever.

Laundry, dishes, Luna's Honey Nut Cheerios, Dad's two eggs over medium with dry toast, coffee, backpacks and newspapers and school projects, more coffee. If she's lucky, Rose, the middle child at fourteen, will have, for once, a sliver of sympathy this morning and offer to help; maybe walking with Luna to school.

"Mom, WAKE UP!" Chloe yells as her declaration that she is entering my room. She places a finger, delicately, under my nose. She gently smoothes my hair back. The attempt at compassion is genuine but short-lived when she pulls the covers off me, exposing me, still in my clothes from the day . . . days before.

She rampages. Heavy footsteps, wildly swinging arms like a scythe through the air, weaponizing the atoms, carving the path where anger flows out, directly toward me. She collects clothes to bring back to the other bathroom, where the laundry closet resides, to start a load of laundry. I roll over and pop open one of my swollen, crusty eyelids, revealing a veiny, traumatized eyeball. I glare at Chloe, sigh and snort into an upright position.

"You look like hell," I mutter as I flutter past Chloe to the bathroom.

"Nice," Chloe says in a whisper. I guess that word won't be making her book-on-tape.

I shut the door and pull on the shower handle, which screeches, starting the flow of water. Before heading in, I peer out into the bedroom. I can see beyond the shower door. Chloe sighs but long enough in order to then inhale the strength she needs to make my bed, as she usually does (only to get rankled later because I so often fall back into it for the rest of the day, unmaking it, again).

She begins to speak, out loud, to the imaginary microphone in the room (maybe even possibly recording it—I wonder), continuing what I extrapolate to be her tell-all book. She has always wanted to be a writer. I am relieved of a smidge of guilt as I justify I'm providing her with content. I can hear her, but I can't make out the exact words. I have to give her that. She has a precise, yet tragic melodic rhythm.

I was awake until 2:30 in the morning waiting for you to come home.

Hell is the new black, Mother. You should know.

By the time you sauntered inside reeking of alcohol, smoke, and that no-good-city scent , with a washed-out face, translucent in texture, the sun was coming up. Your existence, although engorged, holds close to its bony frame, as if to protect your devastated soul, which was once a brilliant flame, and now is a smidgen of a smoldering ash, almost out.

You're a ghost. Gaunt. You have a scar directly below your left eye; it curves downward, a permanent frown contrasting the upturned dark circles under your eyes that hang from the top of your nose to the peaks of your prominent cheekbones. You're thin. You're dirty. The irony, that your name is Grace. There is nothing graceful about you or your nose-dive into self-destruction. You are no more than a hollow shell of your former self. Your chest rises slowly and falls back down into itself. Your breath, a quiet scream, desperate while restrained. It tries to escape, but the shreds of responsibility that remain within you tie it down. You know where you are. You know there is no escaping, and you feel trapped with all of us in this unkempt, untidy, suffocating, unmothered apartment.

It's the idea of reality. The feeling of failure linked together with sobriety that possesses you to feel nothing at all. That tempts you to swallow your feelings; convinces you that the more you swallow, the better you think you feel.

So you can forget you are so selfish.

So you can forget that your presence is really an absence. You become immune from culpability in the wake of forgetting. Because forgetfulness is a mistake. It's a natural human flaw. It happens to old people and dumb teenage boys who smoke too much weed. Forgetfulness is supposed to be a forgivable trait. It would be selfish of me to force you to change. You are a victim to your own flawed, forgetful, human patterns. Somehow you have made us all feel this way about you. That somehow this caustic retreat of yours is earned. That you are entitled to it. So we live "around" you; avoiding, judging, despising and basically numb. God forbid I am, or become, anything like you are now. I need to be everything you are not.

***

"Chloe! I can't find my pants!"

59

That's Luna. The baby. My ten-year-old baby. I turn off the shower, step out and begin to dry myself with my towel. I notice a moldy, damp smell. The towel needs washing. Chloe, I'm sure, avoids gathering it up for the laundry on purpose. To force me to smell a scent branded "disaster."

I can't go back into the bedroom. Not with Chloe there, her dagger still drawn.

Luna, Chloe whispers, putting a quick stop to her rant.

Her call back to reality. Suddenly, geez. God, please. Thank you.

From what I gather, Luna has grown out of her Size 14 kids Gap jeans and will only wear her Target sweatpants to school. She isn't fat, but she has taken to my withdrawal by eating her way to comfort. Too young to act out, like Rose, or take up the reins, like Chloe, but old enough to sense right and wrong.

I see through the crack of the bathroom door that the bed is made. I watch as Chloe sighs, catching her breath. She pushes herself, as if moving against gravity, toward my bedroom door to tend to Luna. I notice she is short of breath, surprising for my two-sport varsity athlete.

"Fuuuuuck," Chloe whispers, again. That one is not making her book either.

"Awwww, damn," Chloe yells from the laundry closet. Luna's sweatpants are still in yesterday's pile of laundry on the floor. "Luna, I didn't get to them."

She grabs the pants, as she throws down the clothes she collected from my floor, and shakes them out.

"I'm 'air' cleaning them now!" Chloe grabs the Febreeze and gives them a spray.

"Good as new Lune."

Chloe walks into their shared bedroom, a bunk bed and a single that gets claimed by the last to bed. She tosses the pants to

Luna.

"Here."

Luna looks up at Chloe smiling as she saves the day. Chloe forces a smile back and heads toward the kitchen to start breakfast. Eggs, coffee, cereal. No milk. There's never milk. Never.

"Luna! Come on! Breakfast."

"Com-ma-ma-ing," Luna yells back, sputtering and then muffling as she puts her clothes on in a mad rush.

"Dad, can you move the paper a bit? That way," Chloe motions toward his left, needing more space at the table, where he's planted his mid-age, thick sausage-like Dad body.

"Huh? Umokaysure," he garbles.

"Why bother responding if you are not going to speak?" Chloe replies with a huff.

"Huh? Um, sure, yesterday's sports section," he doesn't bother looking up. He shakes the paper to the right, clearing space in front of him.

Without time to get the paper this morning from the building lobby, day-old sports isn't his first choice, but it will do. I'm sure she's thinking it beats father—daughter small talk. He's certainly thinking that. Scott has "absent" in his DNA, which became more noticeable after I went MIA.

Chloe fries two eggs and pops a slice of toast into the toaster. She hears him sniff and fidget. He turns a page and shakes out the newspaper, again. She places his eggs and toast on a plate and kisses the top of his head out of habit—this action, rote and meaningless, no longer carries the same affection as when she was young. He doesn't budge but makes a kiss-y sound, blown into the air, to her, but also out of habit. So really, to no one.

Sighing, Chloe returns back to the kitchen counter and pours Luna's Cheerios into her bowl. She'll only eat from the bowl with the smiley face on the front and little blue flowers around the rim. She says it's her magic bowl because the smiley is contagious.

I wish a bowl could make me happy. Chloe wonders.

Luna walks to the table and sits down. Chloe places the bowl of Cheerios and a spoon out in front of her and Luna's eager grin fades. She gazes down into the bowl and picks up the spoon.

"No milk?" She looks up at Chloe as if the sky has fallen.

"Sorry Luna, I'll get more today."

Sorry, sorry, sorry, sorry.

"It's okay." Luna dives into her dry Cheerios as Rose stumbles in. Rose squints, surveying the room.

"Did you make coffee?" Rose asks.

Chloe examines Rose with her bright red lipstick, dark smokey eyes, skin tight shorts, black t-shirt, Doc Martens.

"Well?" Rose inquires, annoyed already. She wakes up annoyed.

"No, I forgot," Chloe says with a tone of resignation as there is never anywhere else "to go" with Rose.

Rose sneers and stomps away. There's a banging on my bathroom door followed by a high-pitched scream, a banshee yell.

"Get the fuck out of the bathroom, Mothership! What are you doing anyway? Why are you doing it? No amount of soap is going to—What? Hello?! Get out! I need something from there. Jesus Christ!" Rose admonishes.

She calls me the Mothership because she says I'm "lost in space." When she initially came up with it, it literally made me laugh. Now that it's been going on so long, it's clearly a sad reminder of my depleted state, my empty vessel. Yes, I'm aware.

After a nanosecond of silence, I turn on the sink faucet to ward off my prey, who I can feel is calculating her next move. Eventually, Rose returns to the kitchen, grabs her bag, and trudges out the door, slamming it hard behind her.

Chloe notices Dad looking up from the sports section, staring after Rose's harsh departure.

Do I clock worry? Nah, couldn't be, Chloe ponders.

Dad retreats back to the newspaper, eggs—safer there.

"Rose!" Chloe says following her, ire spiking.

"Rose!" Chloe yells as she opens the door and swings her body, full-force motion, out around to the elevator to catch her before the elevator arrives.

"Um, Luna?"

With a glare that could kill, Rose stares Chloe down, pods in ears.

"What the fuck, Rose? Your end of the deal. Walk Luna to school!" says Chloe.

The elevator door opens, she slips in, still staring, the elevator doors slowly close, and she disappears.

"Fuck you, Rose!"

"Ah, Chloe said the 'F' word," Luna sings from the dining table.

"You heard no such thing," says Chloe.

"Did too," Luna replies with a giggle.

"Me too," Dad says, winking at Luna.

Luna smiles large at Dad. It's heartwarming for exactly one second.

Chloe comes back to the table, scoops up Luna's hair, and pulls it through her fingers into a high ponytail.

"Rose isn't taking me to school?" Luna peeps.

"No, no, I will. I'll hurry and get ready. You eat," Chloe says soothingly.

"Ow." Chloe pulls too hard on her ponytail.

"Sorry."

"Hi, Daddy," Luna beams his way.

"Loo-oo-ney!" he murmurs, his head buried back in the paper. Chloe waits to see if he will look up at her. No movement.

Chloe finishes Luna's ponytail and sails to the bedroom, new energy, relieved to be momentarily free from the provocation of her dad's inaction and her sister Rose's anger.

Distance. Rebellion. Anger. Denial. Blissful unawareness. Control. If this were a made-for-tv movie, everything could be explained: Rose, the dramatic teenage girl; Scott, the working dedicated father; Luna, the naïve ten-year-old sweetheart; and Chloe, the responsible older sister—that is, if the movie followed the normal narrative where the mother, of course, dies, or is already dead.

But, alas, I. Am. Not. Dead (yet).

"Ready to go?" Luna shouts from the kitchen to Chloe.

"Almost," replies Chloe.

Chloe comes out of the pigsty of a bedroom and sees Luna placing her bowl and spoon carefully in the sink. She does it all without any weight, without any sign of burden or dread. Luna reminds Chloe why to bother every day, her cherubic face a distraction. Her eyes look through Chloe, big and brown. Luna's pudgy little fingers grasp each frontal strap of her backpack like a Scout ready for the hike.

Chloe grabs her keys and her backpack. Luna stops to kiss Dad on the way out. He pulls his eyes away for a moment, puckered lips swiping the air, missing any return, turning his head to watch Luna leave.

Almost, Dad. Nice effort, Chloe ruminates.

The girls head out the building and down the street, walking together toward Luna's school. As they approach, they pass a group of girls huddled around each other. Chloe feels their stares boring into Luna's back. She hears one of them whisper Luna's name and laugh. Chloe glances at Luna. Her face is unfazed except for a tiny wrinkle bunched between her thick eyebrows. Chloe knows Luna heard her name. She links her arm to Luna's and turns and glares back at the girls. The way they stand in a group, all on one leg, the other bent, a flock of flamingos. They see Chloe and avert their eyes swiftly.

When they reach the entrance to the schoolyard, Luna looks up at Chloe. Chloe reaches down for a hug, but Luna stops her. She reaches up toward Chloe's right ear and then back down again. In her small hand, between two cuticle-bitten fingers, is a quarter.

"Ta Da!" Luna sings.

She hands Chloe the quarter, pulls open the door and disappears.

12

"AHHHRRRRRNNNNGGGHHH," I BELCH, as I stretch.

Every morning I wake up with the intention of getting things back to normal. It's there in my head, the will and the anxiety that I ambitiously label ambition. I swear I feel it. I figure if I move my left leg over to the side of the bed, then methodically place my left foot, toes touching the ground for a few minutes, and then *pretend* for a split second that things are okay, I can get some momentum going. Once the other foot hits the ground, it naturally swings my body up. It happens quickly now because I've become so tiny. I can feel my thinness. I can't say I don't like it. It feels right on me. Hollow. I am hollow, much the same as shells that once held life washed up on the beach. The ones that tumble and tumble beyond their control. Rolling, propelled by the waves, the ocean, the tide, which is puppeteered by the moon. Anything can move me.

Hunger visits my body first. A sharp stab of pain in my

stomach, screaming for relief. My mind is trained on dismissal. It is that ache, that cry for attention that sets up for the game. Neurons fire, searching for something to interest me, to fool me, to wake me. I lob a ball into the court of "Let's do it today without taking anything." Then my brain lobs the ball back with a very loud, prominent and practical "Why?" This goes on for a few minutes. I negotiate.

I have enough sense to know that an action, any action, helps me to stop the match game and take the next step. I tunnel my dense body down the short hallway and into the shower. It seems right. I can feel myself coming around, but then there is that pain in my head, *that* headache, and I think about the migraine pills my doctor prescribed. I'm out of them because what they do really well is numb pain caused by a hangover. I depleted those long ago and needless to say I've been blacklisted on refills.

A bang at the bathroom door, followed by an angry muffled voice, brings me out of my head for a moment.

". . . Mothership . . ."

Ah, Rose. The realization of Rose's wrath brings a reflexive regurgitation from the back of my throat, topped with a little bit of acidic vomit as the exclamation.

The muffled voice continues on and concludes with a discernable and prominent "Jesus Christ."

Rose.

The foot stomping communicates her retreat. *That one. That one* is quite the doozy. What a fucking pill *that one* turned out to be. She was the loveliest and most content baby, but then something changed, and she exploded into a walking, talking (barely these days), stomping, fist-pumping, wild-eyed nightmare. I don't know what brought it on. Certainly she was this way before I decided to take a mental vacation. *She*, Rose, is angry. That I get. I see Luna looking at me, and it breaks my heart, but I can't go back to *that life* . . . not yet. I told Scott I needed time. He's not picking up the slack. Luna is holding on, holding her breath—

I'd say figuratively, but quite literally too, because she's blown up into a chunky little monkey—waiting for me to come back. She is a sweet one. I realize she doesn't deserve a mother like me right now, but I can't go there. I won't go there. Right behind Luna is Chloe; arms folded, glaring, accusatory, defiant, disappointed. I can't bear to look at her, and I am sorry that so much has fallen to her. I may be stoned, but I'm not blind. I can't do it. Even *right now* I can't do it.

I listen for the coast to be clear of Rose, and I amble back to bed. I notice the bed is made. *Ah, Chloe, you good girl, you. Mama's good, good girl.* I crawl in and pull the covers up over me. My thinness is my blanket, protecting me. There is solace in comprehending that I could disappear, and it'd be easier for all. Maybe this is a good start.

I do realize that it began with somewhat of a sense of entitlement—the same entitlement I despise in others. People, who I think, are assholes. Entitled assholes. It became me. After my fall, I had prescriptions galore. Easy to get. Then, after my primary doctors started shooing me away, ignoring my calls, turning me down face-to-face in appointments where I feigned pain, I got all my mother friends to supply me. A Vicodin here. Some Oxy there. We *are* our own pharmacy; it's a trade. I didn't see it as an issue. I saw it as a temporary escape. A distraction. I can't seem to *get* back. That world outside my bedroom door keeps churning—all the pieces, albeit broken—in place. Chloe being the damn glue *and* the motor. I suppose I feel guilty, and I do for a minute. Then I don't. I have been sucked dry. I can't do it anymore. I don't care. They are going to have to learn to live without me while I let myself die a little bit, just to keep myself alive.

Sleep comes on strong, a freight train blowing through an empty field in the middle of nowhere, as expected, and while the headache lingers in the back of my head, I know I can, and will, take care of *that*, later.

13

SOLVITUR AMBULANDO—"IT is solved by walking." This phrase refers to the fourth century Greek philosopher, Diogenes's response to the question of whether motion is real—he got up and walked, thus proving motion *is* real.

I concur. Motion *is* real. I question everything else being real. Beginning with myself. I'm disconnected. My will to disappear is more than romantic, it's an obsession. How does one disappear oneself? This is what I am pondering, incessantly, but we humans plant ourselves in creature comforts. I am not above this, nor brave enough to live without it. It is temporary anyway. Some time off.

As it turns out, there are many other problems to which walking is the solution. It is my refuge. I have a plan, things mapped out, always. A zig and a zag through Tribeca, crossing Canal Street into Soho where I worm my way north and south. When I zag my way to Broadway, I head up into the Village and do some fancy zigging along Bleeker and then West 4th. Eventually, I sashay my way around the north end of the Village and then wind my way back down. I never venture above 14th Street in my perpetually high bender. There is no reason to.

There is no other place like New York City. Every block is its own village. I can walk for miles and never hit a freeway, a strip mall, a street without a sidewalk—the mess they made in the suburban sprawl that is the rest of America. I never cross a Walmart, a Target, a Costco, or a BJs. None of those big box shops. No giant car malls. I never see the same color of skin on any person, after person, after person. Various languages falling out of passersby mouths every step of the way. Only in New York City is there magic on every street—each one different. Some old, some new, some change overnight, but it's a constant morph of energy that takes tangible forms. It's the land of dreams and hopes and sorrow and heartbreak, but rarely lack of talent. When it comes to talent, the city sorts it, creates a hierarchy, and usually is correct in its assessment. Even if you are at the bottom of the barrel in New York City, you are still at the top of the game compared to those in a lot of other places. Really. The drive is always here. The raw ambition and the basic fact that almost anyone can tout their game. Sure you get the private school kid who gets that leg up, but it's always fair game for the kid with authenticity from Bed-Stuy. The energy moves. The City that sucks you in taunts you and plays games with your mind, your body, your wallet, your identity, your soul. You fight to stay and keep it going because if you don't, you don't leave, no . . . because you will never come back. No, the more likely scenario is that the City spits you out and you fly to and through your own irrelevance at the speed of light. So, you don't dare ever leave and you don't dare stop.

The air smells of burning leaves, dank fall, musty, with a dash of anything and everything on any given block. My eyes glisten. My body is fluid.

I'm so fucking happy.

THE HOLE IN THE RABBIT

I *am* so fucking high.

Tonight, I start out on the West side of Tribeca. I hit up my friend's place on Harrison Street. Cassie recently had a cyst removed from her back. Nothing special—a fatty cyst. Age. I count on her having scored some great pharms. At my age, there are a plethora of surgeries going on with all our friends—rampant as an airborne virus—voluntary or emergency, necessary or cosmetic. Everyone gets the drugs, and few enjoy taking them for long because of the constipation. New Yorkers, especially, Tribecans don't like to be constipated. That's a given. They don't want their kids to snag the pills either, so typically they have to flush them (which is no longer environmentally friendly) or, more conveniently, I step up, to take them off their hands.

No one seems to mind feeding my habit even though I do occasionally catch the look of pity. Mostly, it's a quick exchange to move me along. I'm not a dummy. They don't want to "catch" what I have. They think it's superstitious and, or, they abide by the Law of Averages, which upholds the belief that outcomes of a random event will "even out" within a group. Really wishful thinking, a bit Schadenfreude, that some kind of balance must occur, an underlying probability of distribution. Like I'm their Jesus. Jesus! They wish. No, no, they hope. Little do they apprehend that the bullets are flying, and each one has a name on it. As long as you keep dodging your bullets, great. Every once in a while, one of them hits. It sucks. It's unfortunate. There is no reason. It's random and chaotic and comes down to luck.

Right now I'm lucky enough to have a lot of friends who are undergoing a lot of surgeries. Out with the fatty cyst. Replace that knee! Shoulder trouble? Fix it. Hip? Eye? Wrist? Fix'em. Colonoscopies. Lumpectomies. Vein removal. Lypo. Eye lifts. Face lifts. Tummy tucks. Boob jobs (a fav of the second wives of male friends—a goldmine of Percs, Vikes, and Oxy). Sad shit, happy new parts, logical upgrades—it's all mine for the simple reason that Lower Manhattan's trophy population's plumbing won't get clogged. God forbid. Their aches, pains and enhancements is my Trail Mix. Keep it coming.

"Chica."

Cassie looks up from the dozens of tiny metal pieces that surround her, "Oh, hey."

"Nice piece," I refer to the bracelet she has in her hand. She's a jewelry designer. Interesting stuff. Gold, diamonds, all "Upscale Hippie." Perfect for this hood, the moneyed Hippies. As my one friend who is nestled on Sutton place refers to Tribecans, "the most down-to-earth snobs you'll ever meet and never know." Liberal and open-minded but precise: your neighbor can be a terrorist as long as he, she or they damn well takes out the garbage *and* recycling. So I wasn't the lowest on the rung of the ladder here. Certainly, others have had the luxury of rehab. I won't. I'm "phasing." It's different.

"So what's up? How are the girls?" Cassie hesitantly exhales.

"Um, good," I say, not really in the mood for small talk. I'm already in full swing.

"And Scott?" Cassie asks.

"Yeah, there . . . check!"

"Yeah, well, at least Scott is around." Cassie says with judgment, peering up from her bifocals, the lenses gaged to make sure she can see the minutiae of beading or linking or soldering.

"Yeah."

"Okay—run along," Cassie squeezes out while trying to meld a very tiny piece of metal to another very tiny piece of metal.

"You kicking me out?" I ask, agitated, but not really *that* bothered. I twist my body around in her little shop. It is very small. I work on balancing so as to not fall into anything. All her pieces are small and precious. Any wrong move, a bump, will dislodge a tray-full of trinket-like, fine-toothed, clinky, dainty, little bracelets, earrings, necklaces with many moons, stars, symbols and stones. Mystical, magical, and Zen for ex-yuppies, who now strive for purpose, hoping to ward off the boring ol' aging process with a collective shield of gold.

"Grace—run along! Or get your shit together. We can all deal with falling down. We all love you. Shit, we supply you. But really, your collateral damage is starting to show," Cassie spews out without missing a beat, not looking up, not pausing, as she applies a tiny bead to the necklace.

"Well, I guess . . . thanks?"

I take off out the door of the two by two foot shop and hoof it down the block.

"Fuck her," I say loudly enough to startle a few passing tourists. I stop briefly at the corner to down a couple Barbies. *Ha, Barbie, that girl from my high school days, the one who started the pool party, the party girl, fitting.* I find a half-empty coffee cup and take a swig to wash them down. I cross the street against traffic, honking, "assholes," but I see the river in front of me, and I head toward it. It's going to be a great walk.

A great walk.

I have not a worry in my head.

14

WALKING FOR DAYS?

It feels that way.

I'm not sure if it's the same day of having just seen Cassie or I've been walking . . . for days. It seems like days. I can't distinguish which day it is today. I'm fairly sure I'm wearing the same clothes, but they feel tight and damp to my skin. I've got the sniffles. It's cold. I cram my hands into my coat pockets, bearing down on the inner linings hard. I'm aware where I am, but time feels as if it's standing still. I can recount a few things. I make my way to my bench by the river. I sit. Exhausted. I remember I had a phone once but can't remember if I've had it recently or how long ago I stopped using it. It doesn't matter.

No one calls.

I sit. It feels good. I have a good view of the water. I see Stuyvesant High School—"Stuy"—to my left. Those smart little fuckers. Such pressure to succeed. Good for them. The list of notable alumni is long. To my right is a ragtag park where a collection of ragtag kids, from all over the city come to hang out. Most of them skateboarders. They are tattered, as if sewn and stitched from craft scraps. Lost kids. Nice kids, but mostly, merely lost. Lost has a tendency of making one, if not mean, then at least jaded. Jaded with a filter on, taking more of the form of a poisonous vapor in the air. You feel it constantly, but it doesn't harm you. The solace they seek, and get from those boards, can generate envy. And good for them too—subverting the pressures of the city, the pressure to succeed. That is to my right.

Makes me wonder which group will end up landing more bodies in rehab. Could be a coin toss.

I see one of the skater boys with a tall boy in a bag. I'm reminded of my plastic bag from the deli placed between my feet. I wish there was a tall boy in mine too. In it is some loose change and the book *Go Ask Alice.* I vaguely recall seeing it on the curbside chucked for garbage pickup. I must have grabbed it. *That* book. To this day *that* book haunts me. I hated it back then. Alice was whiny and ridiculously immature. I remember my teacher, what was her name? Mrs. Neardon? Neidow? Neardon. She had me write my own journal—now somewhere in the depths of my closet. I'm sure it is full of bullshit. That age, those teenage years, were bullshit. So stupid. Everyone was stupid. Poor Pam. She didn't deserve the hand dealt to her. There is that word again, "deserve." Deserve. Just desserts. Does someone deserve their just desserts?

I can't believe the way things went down. Who took the blame. The fault. The coverup. It is buried. Buried under all of us. Her parents smelled something fishy but wouldn't get involved. You keep your place, mind your business, let things fall where they may in every neighborhood, unless you plan on moving and even then, you don't ruffle feathers, cause a stir, or generate alarm. You keep to yourself. Out of despair, grief, they both ended up with soaked livers, living out their final days with alcohol-driven dementia.

So someone was throwing out *Alice*—one of the—what was it? Four million sold? Propaganda at its best. I'm surprised they haven't reprinted it and changed all the drug references to X and meth.

Sooner or later, I was going to have to "come back" and jump back into my old shoes. I knew this, but I wasn't ready yet. I loved the way my little friends made me feel. When mixed with a drink, it was heaven. The ultimate buzz. One way or another, I think, my kids will grow up anyway and have other stuff to deal with. This will plainly give them a running start on how to handle things on their own. No one's childhood is perfect. Not everyone lives a charmed life—in fact, very few do.

My heart aches a bit, not only for my kids, but also for the pains from my childhood. Pam. Dean. Souls that could have been spared but were not because many aren't. It's presumptuous to think anyone has any one thing over another to get a bye. I don't believe in sympathy. It is right in between suicide and syphilis in the dictionary. Right where it belongs. I don't believe in guilt. Guilt is another form of control.

No sympathy. No guilt.

To my right, I hear a familiar laugh.

"Go to hell, you asshole."

It's Rose. I've heard that line one too many times, and it is delivered the same way every time. She has no range. She swiped the hat off a skater boy, and he's chasing her, grabbing her back belt loop. I am too far off in the distance for her to pick me up, but I can see she's smoking a cigarette. A joint is being passed. The slackers. The drifters. There's my Rose. To the right, with the misfits. Her lithe body and swaying stance look elegant, even if she's head-to-toe in baggy hipster gear. She always had the longest, wavy dark hair. It's shiny. She marches to her own drumbeat. She's tough. Someone will break through some day, and I'll be curious to see who does the job. Who takes it on.

Takes her on. *That* I'd like to live to see.

I pop another Barbie and swig from a pint I apparently secured on my travels. Johnnie Walker. Not so bad. Warms me up. I feel the buzz coming on and as my body starts to go limp, I notice a swarm of older kids, tougher in stance and appeal, approach Rose and her beany-headed friends. Money and drugs are exchanged, and as I look closer, I realize that the one guy with the red ski cap and the army coat is the same guy I had secured a few hits from earlier. Today? Yesterday? Really? Rose and I have the same dealer.

I hit this "new low," as they would probably have pointed out if I were to be in rehab, that I am now scoring from the same lowlifes from where my delinquent kid procures. Before it was solely my friends, and then I had my friend's husband, who is a surgeon. He helped me out for a while. This was after I had exhausted my own doctors, who were eventually on to me. I'm sure some kind of alert goes out. There was a crooked doctor from Newark who supplied me for a while, but connecting was a pain in the ass. Similar to New York City real estate, location is everything. I had run out of places to go, and hell, I was probably buying pills my friends were unloading to Red Cap Slim for a bone. It's a vicious circle where everyone wins. Ahhh . . . hell. Rose.

"Rose!" I yelp, like a kicked dog. She hears it and turns first in the wrong direction. She knows it's me, and the look on her face is not surprise, but alarm. I had entered her world. Her turf. This might not turn out well. I see Red Cap Slifty squint my way. He puts his head back down and makes his exit quickly with his posse in tow. Rose zeros in on me. She stands ready to attack. I stay on the bench, sitting up a little bit higher, straighter. The acknowledgment, her acknowledgment, takes a beat to register. I am possibly more stoned than she, and so I think I'm going to "win" this one. Where do I have to go and certainly how does she embarrass me? I have her trumped because I am the stain on her shirt and the smudge of brown on her landscape. I smirk. I can faintly hear her mumbling to her crowd.

"Motherfucker, really? She's here?" Rose says in a shocked, muted tone to her buddies.

In unison, I hear her gang inquire, "Who, who? Who, Rose?" A bunch of chirping birds. Little scrawny scoundrels. All of them.

"I can't go anywhere without her stench following me. She's a no-go mo-fo, and I emphasize, mind you boys, Fucker. No good mom. Never there even when she wasn't a waste-case. Into her own selfish shit. Said she was raised by wolves but I think a she-wolf has better, more instinctive mothering skills. Jeez," Rose howls.

"Aww, Rose, come on, let's go," the gang chimes together, trying to move Rose off her cliff.

"I gotta take care of something first. Hold this," Rose says as she hands her board to the tadpole standing next to her and takes off running. She is galloping my way.

WALLOP.

"Arrrghrrrggg, Mother . . . Rose," I scream.

"You bitch. You cunt. You deserve to die. You motherfuck-ing, non-mother-of-a-fuck, devil of a human being, stupid ass-hole, shithead bitch," Rose screeches as she pummels me. In the distance, I can hear her entourage, yelping, exhaling "oofs" and "whoas" loudly.

My God, such force. She charged me like a bull and, in one furious swoop, slid me off the bench. My head hit the cement and the pounding began. She had me pinned. Her knees nailed down my forearms. Her fists swinging, pulverizing my face.

This is the one who is going to take me down? Not Chloe? *Wow.* Blood, in warm sheaths, is running down my cheeks, and the smashing of bones. Cartilage. My nose. Bones. My cheek. My chin. I can barely see out of my bloodied, battered eye. Her skater boys have gathered, boards in hand, astonished at the sheer might oozing from this tiny silhouette.

"Rose! Rose! Who is this? What the fuck are you doing?" one boy asks.

"It's my mother! My motherfucking mother," Rose cries.

It is the last thing I hear Rose say.

Ha! You little shit. You motherf'ing little shit. Oh my God! The pain! The force! My face! I was not only impressed but also proud. It felt great.

Atta girl.

Then with one swift left, all went black.

15

IT WAS SO clear. The shot was set up perfectly. Oh, that Gerta was such an amazing cinematographer. She danced with her camera. Her fluidity, shot after shot, was so shockingly otherworldly. We had the perfect scene. It worked. Eat your heart out Baz Luhrmann! Danny Boyle! This was my cinematic contribution—this scene—right here. It will be noted. It played out as if it was a dream. The children dancing, the colorful outfits, the grand stage. Palm trees loomed, protecting all who participated. The audience gleamed with excitement, and the teachers and judges were glistening, beads of sweat worn as badges to honor, practice and dedication underscoring the investment. Appropriately adorned ladies and gentlemen were damp and limp from the planning and execution of the event. Four cameras; the best. Direction at its finest. Fifteen minutes of footage. Culminating footage. All the components couldn't have been more in place, meant to be, as if all the stars had aligned at that very moment.

Then . . . then . . . the stage collapsed.

I can feel my face is swollen. My eyes will not open. That

girl, my girl, had really done a job on me. I can feel movement around me. I try to get back to my dream to change the ending, but in reality, it is not a dream. I am reliving a nightmare, a real one. I want to go back. Wish for it to go another way. Wish it away. That was the beginning of the end. Certainly not my fault, but it changed everything. All the parameters, the guardrails, and the purpose fell away. The finals were never finished. The deal was dropped. Hard work, no pay, the promise, the promises—all evaporated. That was it. Just like that.

"Lift up, Miss." I hear. Must be a nurse. Something lifts. Something changes. Clearly a gust of something, maybe morphine, snaked into and through my veins, delivered seamlessly by an IV. Oh mother fucking mother of god . . . THANK YOU. The ghost. She's with me. She is taking care of me. She weaves through my body. We addicts can feel it. Comparable to the moving dot on a smart phone GPS, it moves and slithers into every cell, providing us relief from our own pain. Real or imagined. It doesn't matter. Physical or mental. It doesn't matter. Easily labeled as first world problems. The thing is, we don't care. We are selfish. It is ours. Ours to feel and ours to numb, and we can so easily shut out those who function. They are the bourgeois, the mediocre, the ones who buy into it, the ones who pedal the bike.

"A fool thinks himself to be wise, but a wise man knows himself to be a fool," to quote the big Billy S (as in Shakespear). The cards are dealt, the game is played, but the joke is on them because we *all* get to the same place eventually. There is no prize there. No medal. No trophy. No pat on the back. There is nothing.

16

WHEN I COME to, and can finally open one eye, I realize I am in the hospital. No one is there. No one is waiting to see me. No one is in the waiting room. No one has even called. Footsteps shuffle to the door, it squeaks further ajar, and a nurse comes in.

"Hey there, Mrs. O'Doyle, how ya feeling?" she says with a little bit too much chirp.

I'm not quite sure how to answer. Certainly, the liquid heaven flowing through my veins makes me feel blessed, but I suppose from her view, the bird's eye view, staring down at me in such a way, I look fucked up. My family, fucked up. Everything, fucked up. My life is a little (a *little*? I had to think) in shambles. *How am I feeling? This is the question, right?*

Feeling.

The problem is with the word. I'm not quite sure I'm "feeling."

"I've been better," I mumble through my chapped, pursed lips, tightly held together by the bandages that graced my face.

"I bet you have . . . I bet you have," she replies.

Ah, judgment. Nurse Ratched from *One Flew Over the Cuckoo's Nest*, could it be? Thirty-five years and forty pounds later. Maybe.

"Where—"

"You asked for your friend Pam. That her name?" asks Nurse Ratched.

"Um, Pam? I've . . . yes—" I couldn't remember, but before I could finish pulling up any memory of whatever or whoever I had asked for, she interrupts.

"Yeah, your husband called. He had said a few times he'd be by, but not as of yet. He also informed us that your daughters might stop by. Said there are three of them. Said that the dark-haired one was not allowed here. She's the one that did this, right?" No pause even for me to mumble a reply; she continues, "Can't see that one until you talk to the police. Depends if you are going to file."

Now she pauses.

"Charges."

While my face is smothered in bandages, not a stitch reveals my registered surprise.

Charges? Against my baby? Are you fucking kidding me?

"That's ludicrous," I slur, sounding more like 'Saludiss.' Nurse Ratched understands, accustomed to mangled language of all kinds in her profession.

"Ha, that's sweet! Only a mother's love . . . only a mother's love," she replies either knowingly or sarcastically, or probably both.

"N-n-n-n-n-o. I na ga na duh O a-h," I slobbered out to communicate the best I could, *No, I'm not going to do that.*

"She broke your jaw, mama! She broke your nose! She made your face look like raw hamburger. Heck, she almost broke your neck. Jeeez, whatta ya wanna give her, a medal?"

Tears well in my eyes. I squeeze out, very clearly, "Yes."

17

OOF. IT IS the sound I think I make, but I do not. I thought I did. It is the sound that *I feel.* I feel all over. It is dense and thick and yet encompasses my whole. I am a mummy. This is how a mummy feels.

"She's going to need extra time. Her neck is in traction; those few discs damaged, but without the hoist, she'll need time," the nurse says. I can only make out her silhouette moving from one side of me, my bed, to the other. I feel her moving by me, the warmth pumping from her; and because of her large frame, zaftig, she washes over me, heavy in the air. Her scent escorts her.

"Plus, well, you understand, withdrawal," the nurse says in a softer voice.

"Yeah, I figure," a low, soft voice answers. I struggle to gain consciousness.

Scott?

Days? Weeks? A month? I had lost track of time here in the hospital.

"So the psych nurse was by, offering long-term rehab programs, in or outpatient?" Ms. Scent inquires.

"In," Scott abruptly replies.

"Okay, so yes, well," the nurse continues, "the brochures are there."

Brochures.

I sense the light, the delicate swish of the air from her arm flagging the location of the brochures to the man in the room. I see it in my mind. I intuit where she is pointing.

"Yes," another firm response. It is Scott. I recognize the voice even though it is more subdued than usual, quieter, if that is even possible, but carrying a greater firmness. It might scare me a little if I didn't know Scott better. Our history is too long and interwoven to ever be misconstrued or feared. He can sense weakness. One can't be vulnerable with Scott.

We know where the other buried the bodies.

We helped each other bury them.

***

His Irish Travellers' blood runs deep.

Scott's family was totally different from mine. They acted as if they were straight-laced and clean-cut, but everyone knew better. You don't work labor relations for Chicago unions and *not* have to work hard at keeping everyone's dirt (or your own, for that matter) under the rug—*every ghost in its specified closet.* His mom was a prim, petite housewife and she kept a perfect house. There were seven kids including Scott who was the oldest and often had to look after the others, always helping his mom. He always offered. That's the kind of guy he was. All the kids dressed impeccably—iron-pleated trousers, dress doilies pressed flat, broaches, handkerchiefs; exactly so. He had a sister next, Katie, who everyone thought was his fraternal twin because they were in the same grade. Scott became extremely sick one year and had to repeat third grade—proof that they were not twins, but no one listened to the facts. There were two sets of identical twins—the first set of identical twin girls. I didn't ever think it was worth learning their names. I never remember who was who. Next came the identical boy twins—same thing about the names. Finally, last *and* least, literally, the scrawny little baby, Ian. It was as if decent-sized babies had been exhausted and this "model" was all they had left. Ian was forever sick and thus forever small.

Scott's father was an O'Doyle. He liked to remind everyone all the time, "O'DOYLES DON'T DO ANYTHING . . . I SAID ANYTHING! . . . HALF WAY!" (The only exception to that rule was Ian evidently.) Scott's mom was called Sissy. I never found out her real name. She brought the Irish Travellers descent to the lineage, and while she was the mouse next to the elephant that was Mr. O'Doyle, she also wielded the power to make him tiptoe around any family matter with some degree of fear. Make no mistake, she was the boss.

She shook her head and smiled when Scott's father bellowed from across the room, where he'd sit sipping his nightly Scotch before nodding off.

"HALF WAY TO YOUR DREAMS IS WHERE YOU ARE JACK!" she'd yell back with the tonsils of a cheerleader. Sissy's replies made no sense at all, but that was normal. Her mind worked in its own way, often taking the scenic route around any topic or discussion. By the time anything poured out of her mouth, it had been dismantled to something completely nonsensical and illogical to the rest of us, including Jack, who however, always laughed at her and told her she was so "clever."

The kids broke down the middle, half pale and blonde with blue eyes, and the other half more dark complected with black hair and brown eyes. Always clean and scrubbed, matching the rest of the house, which was so clean you could eat off any floor. However, every family has its own form of dirt or "pollution," and in the O'Doyle family, the spillage came in the form of noise. Everyone was yelling all the time, even about the slightest things.

"I'M GOING OUT!" was yelled at the top of any set of O'Doyle lungs, even if no one was home to hear it or no one cared.

"I'M LOOKING FOR MY OTHER SOCK."

"I'M GOING TO TAKE A SHOWER."

"WHERE'S THE CHEESE?"

"WHAT CHEESE?"

"THE CHEESE!"

"WHO'S SOCK IS THIS BY THE BREAD BASKET?"

Everyone yelling, all the time. Everyone except Scott. Scott was as quiet as a mole. He said nothing; simply nodded, helped out, and went about his business. Dinner was a time of silence because everyone was shoveling food on plates and into mouths—too busy eating to talk (except Ian who was always too sickly to eat, but he conformed nonetheless, keeping his lips sealed).

Scott's mom was never fond of me. She narrowed her eyes on me, throwing darts of suspicion from the minute I set foot in the house to the minute I left. She was on constant alert that at any moment I was going to pocket one of her Lladros or something; as if they would even fit in my pocket. She had hundreds of them. She'd know if one went missing as there was a method of madness to their presentation. She thrived on order. With all the yelling and running and wilding, I'm surprised a few of them didn't end up shattered into pieces. I'm sure if they ever did, she'd have found a way to blame me.

She knew who my siblings were; she knew the reputation my

parents had. She wasn't too pleased with what she saw in me. My family were sailors. This equated to partiers. A bit rambunctious. My dad accidentally driving his Coupe de Ville Caddy into Lake Michigan wasn't the greatest publicity move he could make to garner new business or make new friends—at least not the right ones right away. Thank God, I guess, he wasn't too drunk to slither out the window as the car sank to the bottom— only about eight feet deep around that turn. Better that he was alone so no one else got hurt. He never even retrieved that car. This sort of "move" served as a catalyst to attracting rather than repelling business. It solidified his legendary status among the other partying natives of Chicago. This act alone upset Mrs. O'Doyle, and not because he almost killed himself. She was miffed about the flagrant disregard of a luxury item, a privileged purchase one "achieves" with hard-earned money—that upset her. I didn't necessarily disagree with this, but God as my witness I had no control over my family, and I wasn't about to start taking the rap for them. I realized early on with regard to family, we share the same gene pool, and the same spatial plane in life, for a while, but that's it. Like a ship full of passengers, everyone is sailing the same sea, taking in the same sky, out of the same port, but checks into his or her own cabin. No matter how many are on board, it never fails; there are always fewer life jackets than passengers, compelling some to go without and committing to going down with the ship (should that happen).

This was my family.

We all loved and hated each other with equal passion. So instead of fighting for life jackets, it was more our nature to try to sink the ship and fight about who was to go down with it.

I was aware of the kind of girl Mrs. O'Doyle wanted for her son. I was not her. This bothered me a little bit but not a lot. Her son was free to be attracted to whomever he wanted to be attracted to, and I couldn't help that it was me. So I let it go. I was very nice to her and Mr. O'Doyle. Always respectful. I babysat those kids, along with Scott, so much that one time when Scott was upstate hunting with a friend, they called me to watch the brood on my own. They never came home to the house as they left it—with or without Scott. When we had to watch the little ones, we did art projects, baked, danced and created outfits. I'd often use Mrs. O'Doyle's flowers (placed all over the house) and popcorn, and other finds, stringing up head wreaths for the girls and hippy necklaces for the boys. The yelling continued when the parents were out (except of course, for Scott).

"MAKE THAT FOR MY HAIR," twin girl #1 yelled.

"ME FIRST!" bellowed twin girl #2.

I had to really work hard to take a hit off a roach out the basement bathroom window. I'd tell them I was pooping to which, when the door opened, they'd scream about the smell which was merely the overuse of Lysol. Or, I would send them off on a scavenger hunt to do a quick shot or two of Jack's scotch. Unlike Sissy's Lladros, Jack never measured or even noticed.

Not too late, Scott's parents would come through the door. Mr. O'Doyle would yell "HEY, KIDS! WE'RE HOME."

"HOW WERE THE KIDS, KIDS?" Sissy . . . yelled.

"Good," we'd reply simultaneously, smiling at each other, knowing now we could finally steal away to go make out.

We couldn't, and Scott would never, show any public display of affection to me or toward me in front of his siblings. One time he held my hand, and they "EWE'D" and "YUCKED" for hours. They put on an entire theatrical performance "EW-ING" and "YUCKING." As we could never get them to bed, the minute the parents walked through the door, they all yelled, "OH MY GOSH, SCOTT HELD GRACE'S HAND AND IT WAS SO GROSS," falling over each other, trying to be the first to tell Sissy how entirely, *really, really* gross it all was. "IS THAT ALL HE HELD?," she replied. The kids held their tummies, giggling and faking vomit noises.

At first, Sissy was laughing too, but then her expression shifted. As the gags and giggles faded, so too did her smile, and suddenly she couldn't look at me. She beelined right to the kids' floral accessories and gathered them up, and then, with a warm towel in hand, scrubbed their faces, arms and hands, sterilizing them of anything that might have fallen off me and onto them. We caught each other's eyes. She dished it. I took it. Scott observed it. Jack avoided it, sauntering to his den to pour a nightcap and watch the local news (shootings, Chicago. There was never a night without one).

***

Now, beside me, I can feel Scott. I will my head toward him, prying my eyes open, my eyelashes interlaced and glued with phlegm, only a tad bit so he can see me, see him.

"Who knew our spider of a girl packed that much punch?" he says, as one would expect, quietly, very quietly, as if he's talking to himself. Though I can barely see through my mucus-eyed veil, he has a smile on his face.

"Oof," I blow out of my mouth in reply, quietly.

PART III
Tribulations
New York City

18

WHEN YOU DON'T have guns, you don't dream about them. When you do, you do.

When you have a swimming pool, you never think, *Ah, yes! That's where I will drown one day.*

But when you have a gun, you always think, *Will this gun kill me someday?*

I clock his new Glock on top of the credenza.

Scott's arsenal has grown exponentially over the years. Now that I am back, under house arrest, so to speak, I notice.

He already had quite the repository of weaponry prior to my escapade of debauchery. He inherited his father's collection, added to it, and is now taking it to a new level. A highly guarded storage unit, specifically for this type of armory, with an unknown address and underground facilities in New Jersey, keeps the goods, similar to wine, at the right temperature and moisture-free. He belongs to a club over there where the laws are lax on what you can own and shoot. He also visits a friend's upstate place for regular target practice.

Today, thirty days home and sober, there is a change in the air. A change in the mood. My mood. Scott asks the girls to join him at the club and then stay overnight upstate with his friends. I overhear them readying to go.

"Will I be able to shoot that new gun?" Rose inquires excitedly.

"Sure," says Scott, the man of few words.

"Can we do a contest?" Luna asks.

"Sure."

"A . . . a . . . are we just leaving Mom h. . . here?" Chloe chimes in, nervously.

"Yup."

The collective thought is that a gun collection, called an arsenal, is amassed by the continuous expansion of the "sport" of hunting. That one takes up the sport or is born into a family that hunts. Scott's family started as bird hunters and then graduated to larger animals. Their history of running guns is never discussed. That is how it started, but one can draw the lines back into history to no end. This family or any other family. "Hunting," today, is the sheer curtain to a window into the past that was blacked out long ago.

The dirty truth is that shooting a gun releases dopamine, the brain's most efficient and effective messenger. Engagement. Excitement. Creativity. Desire. Emotion. Pattern recognition. Risk. Risk. Risk. The brain and heart rate, blood pressure, and muscle reactions thrive on this thrill and skill booster. There is want. Want. More. Better. Higher. Farther. Further. Faster.

Sounds familiar.

Scott and I have more in common, but not "more than we

know." Nope. We know. *We know.* Addiction. Scott is addicted to guns. I remember *that* day, the accident, when Scott's father's armory in the trunk was kept on the down low by the Chicago police. How can it not seep into your dreams? It seeps. Nonstop. Like a junkie's runny nose.

Drip.

Drip.

Drip.

"Okay, so Luna. Starting with you . . . ," Scott says as he starts moving their day packs from various areas of the apartment to the front door, "throw my way a gun safety rule!"

"Never point the gun at anything you're not going to shoot!" Rose yells from her room as she frantically throws clothing into her backpack.

"That is correct but is your name Luna?" Scott fires back. "Loonie?"

"Um . . . ," mumbles Luna.

"Always think a gun is loaded!" Chloe belts out from the kitchen while gathering food for the outing.

"Correct, but you are not Luna," Scott answers, losing patience. "Lune?"

"Um . . . ," Luna continues to mumble.

"Oh, oh . . ." Rose comes into the living room and throws her bag on the pile, "keep your finger off the trigger until you are ready to shoot!"

"Geez . . . Luna!" Scott shouts.

"Um . . . , " Luna says more clearly. "Be sure of what you're shooting at."

"Bingo!" Scott belts out. "And what's beyond it, right?"

"Yes!" Luna, Rose, and Chloe scream happily in unison.

With everything gathered at the front door, I listen to them through the crack in my bedroom door. There are less than heartfelt mumblings of goodbyes, not really aimed at me, to me, or for me. Often said into thin air to relieve them of the obligatory motion of a farewell.

For all they care, I'm simply a reminder of the hell they've had to endure in the past few months.

19

THE TRIGGER IS squeezed, releasing the firing pin, which moves with great force. The firing pin strikes the primer. The primer is the chemical or device responsible for initiating the propellant combustion. The spark from the primer ignites the gunpowder. Gas converted from the burning powder rapidly expands in the cartridge. This will push the projectiles out of the gun barrel, causing them to explode.

When bullets fly through the air, they *go* superfast. Amazingly fast. The fastest bullet can speed more than 2,600 feet per second; over 1,800 miles per hour. Compare that to driving a car at 60 miles per hour. Or flying in a plane at 300 miles per hour. Comparison is unfathomable.

The most accurate shooting is done with the dominant eye, or "master" eye. This is usually the same as your dominant hand, but not always, and should be determined before "sight-in" on the rifle or handgun. It is interesting that closing one eye, the less dominant eye, lowers the activity of the half of the brain that isn't technically being used. This frees the rest of the brain from distractions, helping to line up the target more easily.

Today, I am choosing to *close* both eyes. I am shutting down *both* sides of my brain that I do not want, "technically," in use. The house is quiet. I am alone. Alone. There is a list. A lot of lists. Lists created to keep me busy. To *not* think about wanting to get high. To not speed 1,800 miles per hour.

The city is quiet. It is a Sunday, which is always much more pleasant with regard to noise. While it is nice to be home, my surroundings, typically familiar, feel distant. My face is better, but I'm still scarred. I still have two more days before Scott is to drive me north to rehab. This is the deal we struck in order for me to be able to come home for a stretch. I'll be headed to an inpatient facility—"community," they prefer to call them—"up north." Maine, Vermont, New Hampshire, or Canada. Scott chose the option but is not telling me in fear that I might hatch an escape plan. I'm sure he has made sure it is in a state far enough away to guarantee there is no showing up on the door-step without at least an eight-hour warning. I have only two days to "get it all in." All good things must come to an end. This is when it is supposed to all end, anyway.

I will have my rehab, put together the pieces, and get up and going again. First, I have forty-eight hours and to hell if I was going to sweat it out in bed. I have been waiting for this final window, and this is my chance.

(1,800 miles per hour.)

I head out to the hallway, but I stop cold and turn around and go back in. I do this over and over again, several more times. But I come back. I never lock up the door. It is open. I start over. And over. And over again. And again. And again. And again.

(1,800 miles per hour.)

I head back to the bed and lie on top of it, holding myself, as if I'm my own straight jacket. I hold on tight. I breathe and try to be mindful. I concentrate on starting a list.

When I went through detox, after all the nausea, vomiting, headaches, high temperatures, body aches, spasms, chills, heart palpitations, profuse sweating, shaking, tingles, tremors, restlessness, depression, insomnia, fatigue, anxiety, cravings, mood swings, clammy skin, deliriousness, seizures, and hallucinations subsided, I began to make lists to keep busy. To distract. To survive.

Here is one list:

    1. Spring-clean the whole house. One room at a time.

        a. Living room

        b. Family room

        c. Bedroom

        d. Bathroom

        e. Second bathroom

        f. Girls' room

        g. Rose's room (will she let me in?)

        h. Basement

        i. Closets in each room where stuff is stored

    2. After that, start in one room and go shelf by shelf. Decluttering.

        a. Make three piles.

            i. keeping

            ii. giving away

            iii. throwing out

    3. Repeat in each room. Checkmark progress.

Here is another:

    1. Go in the closet and go through old clothes to give away.

2. Do the same in the shoe closet.

3. Sit down with each girl and do the same (steps 1 and 2 above).

And another:

1. Go into plastic bins and scan and organize writing on the computer.

2. Tear apart photo albums and go through which photos to scan. Scan photos and put them on the computer. Share with girls.

3. Go through digital photos and organize on the computer. Share with girls.

And another:

1. Clean out the basement.

2. Winterize deck.

3. Layout and mark and price all costume jewelry for family distribution and/or sale.

4. Box up the camera collection and put it in the basement.

5. Sort through books and put them on bookshelves in an organized way.

Not another.

I start none of the above. Instead, I check my phone to no avail for nothing. I scan the news. None of it is good. I roam from room to room wondering "where to start," never to start.

I itch.

I bite my cuticles.

I pick at food—here and there.

I walk around and talk to myself.

I decide to dust. Every room. I think about that for five minutes before I actually pull out the duster and the Pledge. I look at both items. I put them away. I'll dust tomorrow.

I decide I'll vacuum tomorrow too. Or wait until I dust and then plan to vacuum.

I'll start a cleaning chart and work my way around the house.

I go on the computer to start the chart. Instead, I Google all the people I used to work with; checking out what they are doing now.

Ah, yes, her.

Oh, OH, him. Wow.

Shit! Him.

Dead.

What?

Dead.

Bitch.

Fuck. Real bitch.

I get depressed.

I bite my cheek.

I pick at my elbows.

I itch.

I bite my cuticles. They bleed.

I scratch.

I run a bath.

I take a bath.

I think. And think. And think.

I want to stop thinking.

(1,800 miles per hour.)

I don't hear anyone. I never heard any door open. Are they here? Still here? Did they go out? Why are the girls not checking on me? They are not home? Are they not coming back? Are they stopping for dinner somewhere? Did they go overnight? I feel dizzy. I hear voices.

I towel off my body, methodically mopping up any moisture up in a circular massaging motion. I have time. So much time.

I head to my bed. I pick up my iPad. I try to read a book I had downloaded eons ago. Instead, I start going through the newsfeed again. I put down the iPad. I look at my phone for a second. No calls. No texts. It's become late, too soon. 6:44 p.m. I guess I could get up and eat something, watch some TV, and then go to bed early. I fold to my side in fetal position and I sigh. I try to cry. I can't. I want to cry. I try to think about all the sad things in my life so that I will cry. Nothing.

I close my eyes. I listen to the city.

Tomorrow.

Repeat.

And so on.

1,800 miles per hour and another day to go.

20

REDEMPTION. THE ACTION of saving or being saved from sin, error or evil. Saving. Vindication. Absolution. Clearing a debt. Retrieval. Recovery. Reclamation. Repossession. Recoupment. Return.

Not happening.

There is a documentary called *Some Kind of Monster* about one of the biggest rock bands of all time, Metallica. They are having issues similar to those of being in a marriage and decide, in order to keep the band together, they need therapy. They were trying to get their album, *St. Anger,* produced and distributed precisely at the same time their bassist quits and their frontman enters rehab for alcoholism—or *maybe* it was solely a drinking issue. The therapy lasts hundreds of days and the film marks each day in the lower third (i.e. the text at the bottom of the screen). It's excruciating. It's done intentionally, so you *feel it.*

To anyone who knows about quitting anything, going cold turkey, doing it on one's own, or with help, it is a minute by minute, hour by hour, day by day, week by week, month by month and year by year process. Ordeal is a more fitting word. It is a mindfucking, numbing ordeal making the days blend. The monkey on your back clings tight, not numb or dull, but instead piercing.

Counting is a big part of it. Counting steps, stairs, cars, horns. Doors in the building slamming. Clicks of something in the apartment—clicks that always clicked, but now I count the clicks. Counting minutes until a meal—any meal, breakfast, lunch or dinner—but no snacks. Transference of pleasure is expected. From a buzz, to the taste of food, to the focus on something in the street, to the feeling of shower spray on my skin, everything intensified. Maybe not so much intensified, but there is a need for intensification. So, whether it is real or not, this transference feels real. It feels necessary. It is desired. Therefore, routine, redundancy and consistency matter. Monotony sets in. When this happens, the trading starts to happen. Making deals with God. The bartering begins. Same as when someone close to you is sick. You start to barter with God to do this for that. Start going to church if you'll, say, just "let her live." Or you'll give up smoking and the booze; just "don't let him die."

In my case, starting small seems less insulting to God.

If I can just, maybe, sleep a little longer, I will make up for it tomorrow when I'm exercising.

If I skip exercising tomorrow, I'll double up on the household chores in addition to the exercise hour.

If I can just smell the scotch in the bottle. Just smell it. I'll not smell it again.

It begins to build.

And build.

And build.

It starts with a hum. An underlying vibration.

It gets louder.

And louder.

And louder.

LOUD.

HUM.

My head hurts. My eyes burn. Thirty days? Forty? I'm to do this 'til ninety? 'Til 120? 180? 365? 365 times two, times three, times forever? 'Til I'm dead? I'm going to live like this?

(1,800 miles per hour.)

Where is everyone?

What time is it?

Where's the shot glass? I'm just going to drink some diet ginger ale from it. Scott didn't put a lock on the liquor cabinet. I open it up. The bottles are glistening, center stage.

This reminds me of the cartoon when I was young, where Tom, the cat from Tom and Jerry, got sloshed from drinking from a jug marked "XXX." He wobbled and stumbled, drunk, and the bottles of spirits literally came alive, as spirits, and danced around him. This is how these bottles appear to me. My friends. Beckoning me to play. To come hither. To imbibe. I stand there mesmerized. Yearning. Beyond yearning. It is a magnetism so strong that I am in a trance, staring. I think about where there might be any, any pills in the house. Anything. Does Rose have any drugs hidden? She'd be the one who might have any in her room. The inside of my head runs a high-speed ping pong game with 20 balls in play at once. I am losing any sense of strength, courage, resiliency. It is all on me. Up to me. Right then and there. No policing me. No babysitting me. As family and friends know, with someone beating an addiction (or two . . . or more), the addict has to want it. Want it enough to keep going, second by second, minute by minute, hour by hour, day by day, week by week, month by month, year by year, decade by decade.

Until death.

It is some fucking way to live.

No fucking way to live.

***

The universe works in mysterious ways. I remember seeing a set of keys on the credenza by the door. I vaguely remember that Chloe was caring for the 5th floor neighbors' cats this week.

I sit straight up. I take note, possessed. This is the moment when the executive decision-making process surprisingly becomes rational. Clear. It is the tipping point. The point of no return. There is no question, as I envision my plan. I am going to take those keys, to check on the cats, of course, in Chloe's absence, since she's off shooting with Scott. I'm going to go check on those cats. And I do.

Water in the cat bowls. Enough dry food in their food bowls. Litter box. Fuck their shit.

Dewars on the booze trolley by the sliding door. Vicodin in the med cab. Three twenties on the counter, no doubt for Chloe. Because she is the good girl I know her to be, she won't take it 'til the neighbors hand it to her, and even then she'll only take one bill. So I take it all.

The cats are fucking fine.

21

THE WOMAN LEANS down with a soft fluffy toy in hand, shaking it and rubbing it on her newborn granddaughter's belly. The baby coos softly, calmed by the touch. When she pulls it away to shake again above the baby's head, the baby flails its arms and legs in jerking motions, what babies do with that kind of energy. Nestling the plush toy back on the belly, the baby settles once again. The woman has a hair color hard to explain (as post-Red often is). With her slight frame, almost petite, she hovers over the child.

"I've had a glass of wine, or I'd hold her," she says.

"Mom, you can hold her even after one glass of wine!" her daughter says laughing.

The daughter's husband comes into the room. A fire burns bright in the fireplace giving the room a cozy glow. Over the fire is a mantle. On the mantle are several nicely framed photos;

some large and some small, but the largest one stands out. It is a family photograph. There are more than ten people in the photo. Maybe twenty? I can't see that far into the house, but I can see enough; it is a very large family. Front and center is the matriarch. Pam. It's Pam.

There is a knock on the door. The daughter's husband opens it. It's a dark-haired fellow, his ponytail hanging a little too long for his age, marking him as somewhat of an outlier. He doesn't fit the knit sweater and docker crowd with his worn jeans and black jean jacket, and floppy canvas shoes—not a stitch on him warm enough for this weather.

"Hey you! Come on in!" yells Pam from across the room.

"Hey," Dean replies softly, handing a bag with a box of store-bought cookies to the daughter's husband, who pats Dean on the back, giving his shoulder a squeeze before taking the bag and walking toward the kitchen. Dean returns the exchange of care with a few shoulder taps as well. Pam walks over and gives Dean a strong, long, tight hug. She holds onto him, tucking her head into the nape of his neck. When she lets go, he sighs.

"Come on in. Come in by the fire," Pam says. "What'll you have? A Coke? Fizzy water?"

"Diet Coke, you have?" Dean replies quietly as if contemplating other offerings but immediately stays in his lane sticking to his known script of health and recovery.

"Sure," says the daughter's husband.

Dean walks tenderly to the cradle, erected in the living room for such visits, having had double below-the-knee amputations due to slow healing wounds from diabetes.

"Ah, this is number 8!" he almost whispers.

"Yes! Lucky 8. Christina." Pam replies melodically, looking right at the baby.

"Wow, who would have thought? Right?" says Dean.

"I know. Me! Right? I had the highest batting average of scaring all the boys away!" shouts Pam.

"You never scared me," Dean declares.

"Please!" Pam says.

"I somehow couldn't ever catch you, your mom," Dean says as he glances the way of the child's mother. "Your grandma," Dean says as he looks down at the cooing baby.

The scene starts to melt. Like a photo taking to fire, everything starts to burn and blend, bright colors, orange and red and the yellows. The flames! It is magnificent. I put my hand up to the window to try to feel the heat. There is none. Nothing. Nothing but cold.

"M'am," a doorman calls out to me.

"Huh?" I respond with confusion.

"M'am, Miss, are you okay?" the doorman asks.

"Um . . . I . . . yes, I'm so sorry. Yes."

"Okay, well then . . . " Doorman.

"Yes, yes." I walk away.

22

I WALK A couple more blocks and see another lit window. It draws me in. It's a small room with four men sitting in front of a television set hung in the corner of the room, up above, beyond reach. A news show is on. There is some banter back and forth between the men, low-key arguing. The man in the wheelchair, who wields the remote, changes the channel to another boldly bellowing news show.

The walls are stained yellow, and the posters rimming the room, haphazardly hung, are tattered, the tape holding them precariously to the wall has hardened and is a darker yellowing than the walls. A halfway house is my guess. Certainly not the decor I witnessed at Pam's daughter's house.

I see Dean there.

The TV is loud. The news is covering a story about a man who saved another man's life.

"The courageous man, Dean Karney, jumped into the river, swimming to the older man who had jumped in minutes before, and wrapped him in a lifeguard hold, bringing him to shore," the news anchor says with accompanying video of the rescue.

The man in the wheelchair clicks the remote back to the former news channel. Again, it's a story about Dean.

"He fled from his car and ran to the older gentleman on the ground, who apparently had had a heart attack, and began administering CPR. This complete stranger!" the talking head proclaims again, with video of the heroic act for all to see.

"Apparently, Mr. Karney," the newsperson continues, "worked full-time at an assisted living center but was laid off months ago and came upon hard times."

"Humpff," Dean smirks at the television, and he abruptly gets up and walks out of the room and into the next room. That next window is lit, and I move over to it.

This is his room. In 8 x 8 feet fits a twin bed, made to the tee with nurse's corners no less, a small dresser, a pillar-size closet and a desk with a chair. There are no photos on the wall, not even a motivational poster. There is one book on his desk, but I can't read the title on the spine. It is a hardcover book.

Dean sits on the end of the bed. He puts his face in his hands and breathes a heavy sigh. He slumps over, embracing himself in a hold to keep him there, frozen.

Dean did not have an easy upbringing. When he finally connected with Pam it was a blessing for him. Even though she herself was a wild one, she came from a very sturdy family, and that structure helped Dean. In fact, while he and Pam were quite the item, in hindsight, he was probably more in love with gaining the family than having the girlfriend.

His family began with a father shot outside an Old Town bar. A mother, who (with eight kids) couldn't do more than drink her sorrows away. Dean got the shit kicked out of him, as he was the runt, but was born smack dab in the middle of the swarthy brood. Any brother who was not in prison or described often in vague terms as "away for a bit" or "visiting an uncle" saw it fit to take him down. The sisters, while sympathetic, were busy looking for loves capable of whisking them far away, or at least out of that house.

Dean inherited one thing that no one else did—a compassionate heart. He gave that heart in full, even though he hung with that motley crew. All the while as the king of delinquency, he was always chivalrous with girls and women, and Pam was the main recipient of this chivalry. It overflowed to her friends (me), and surprisingly, even his male friends. Back in the 70s, because so many families were on the brink of flat-out falling apart in all ways (emotionally, physically, financially), friends became family.

Dean was there—the stoic, righteous book end, the period of a sentence. Always there to help, to hold, to accept, to confront if forced, to take the heat. Until he wasn't.

The window light fades slowly on my scene as a man walking a large dog comes up the street and breaks my spell. I turn to him and the dog and watch them pass.

"Evening," the guy says, a common gesture to quell the fear of two strangers passing by on a deserted street in the city.

I don't reply. I nod. He walks on.

When I look back at the window, it is dark.

The room is dark.

The whole building is dark.

23

DOPAMINE CIRCUITRY HAS an inborn timing mechanism. It evolved in the human brain due to danger and immediacy, when threats, and rewards of those threats, were signaled in the food chain. If the reward follows the stimulus by roughly 100 to 200 milliseconds (that's .1 to .2 seconds)—POW!

That's dopamine's sweet spot.

Firing a muzzleloader between multiple firings takes too long to create a reward loop. Firing an automatic weapon? Sweet spot. A round fires every 100 milliseconds. Guns are addictive. Assault weapons are far more addictive than most.

"I've got a new baby to try," Scott tells the girls as they stand by his side at the shooting club. "This one is a Ruger 10/22, pistol grip. A good starter for you all."

"Hmmm," Chloe responds, unsure, clocking her surroundings at the club.

"With accuracy and no recoil, really, the Ruger is perfect for you girls—your aim, shot, your marksmanship. Hitting the target."

"Huh?" Luna replies, pulling a lollipop out of her mouth. Her fingers are sticky. Scott notices this, making a mental note to eventually tell her to wash her hands, but not yet. Let her enjoy herself, he thinks.

"Don't worry though. I've got the Glock and the regular .22 too. A variety today. You'll for sure have a favorite." Scott says somewhat upbeat.

"I want the little one," Luna replies.

"The .38 special?" Scott says as he winks at Luna. "We left that little girl home today." Luna responds by making a sucking noise, SMACK, as she pulls the lollipop from her puckered mouth. Scott laughs. Luna is very happy to make her dad laugh, and so she laughs. The vibe is nice. Everyone is calm, setting up to shoot.

"Yeah, give me that auto-baby," Rose purrs, cutting into the moment of peace.

"Shouldn't we check in on Mom?" Chloe says, interrupting the flow of conversation.

"Here, take your muffs," Scott says, pointing to the headphone gear to protect their ears. "Let's get set up."

"So, this is the one to use for self-defense?" Rose asks.

"Hello?" Chloe.

Scott looks at Chloe for a nanosecond and turns toward Rose to answer her question.

"Well, that depends. In general, the .22 doesn't penetrate very deeply. Doesn't make a big hole. So that takes blood loss out of the equation," Scott replies. "And many factors go into how, how far, and where a bullet travels. Like wind, obstacles, the weight of the bullet and trajectory."

"And so?" Rose.

"Yeah, well, closer range, you want the Glock. Something say, coming down the road, you're gonna like this," Scott replies, holding up the Ruger, "the scope, yeah, precision." He rubs the shaft, genuinely fond.

It is scientifically known that the first true taste of a dopamine rush is always the best. After that, there are diminishing returns. The first time someone snorts, say cocaine, it feels so amazingly . . . amazing. Then, after that, not so great. One will basically keep upping their use to try to get back that original high—that amazingly amazing. Because this is not ever possible, it becomes a vicious cycle.

The same goes for guns. Addicts are addicts, regardless of the drug. This purest of pure desire then escalates and does more damage, causes more harm and increases over time. It feels like lightning would feel if you could feel lightning in your blood, your veins, the strike on the brain, the bombardment on the welcoming neurons.

Nothing travels faster than an assault rifle bullet, except lightning.

24

A COUPLE SPEEDBALLS.

I rinse my mouth with some Johnnie Black. It's like mouth-wash. My tongue and every taste bud welcoming it.

Red Cap Slifty on a messenger bike in about five minutes. Fast. Looks similar to that speed skater, Apolo Ohno. He rides away as fast as he came.

I want to pace myself. This is the one last stroll. There is a brisk breeze at dusk. It washes over my face, engulfing me, walking me on the path to a new beginning. I can feel it. Things are going to get better now. The first speedball comes on strong. The lights blend into beautiful bands of color. The city is putting on its very own light show for my farewell before I head to rehab. I hear music in the distance. New York City is in liquid form, raging through my body, mind and soul—a river rushing over stones. It is beautiful. No pain. No motherfucking pain. Only peace.

I turn the corner and mosey my way down Franklin Street, wobbling from loading dock to loading dock, grabbing onto the rim when I need to propel myself in forward motion. Heading toward Greenwich Street, I see in the distance a familiar outline. I can tell by the way his shoulders are bunched up around his ears—it's Scott. My beloved Scott! Always here to rescue me. From day one at Tony Jr.'s party to today, this moment. This day always comes. I move closer but I slow up. He is not happy. He's neither mad, nor sad. He is . . . nothing. Is this Scott?

"S-s-s-scott?" I inquire. "Whatttruuu? Whaaaa . . . ?"

In his nothingness, he lightly takes my arm, and we walk south toward the community college parking garage. Not a word is said. At least not from him to me. *I think* I try to speak again, but my words drop out, PLUNK, PLUNK, hot potatoes falling from my mouth, each one more mispronounced than the one before, and they string together like bad taffy. I take another swig of my Johnnie. I half-heartedly offer it to Scott who looks my way and scoffs. He is pulling me along on a mission but we are no longer headed back to our apartment.

At the corner, he searches my pockets and finds my second speedball gel cap, in a clear snack-size baggy. He pockets it.

"Noooo, Sssco-tt," I protest. "It's my last night. Lassst time."

He grabs my arms and drags me, quick and rough, into the parking garage, into the corner, behind an extra-large SUV, a Tahoe or something. Black. Dark. Cold. Out of sight of any security cameras. He fumbles around in his coat pocket, grabbing something—a different gel capsule, it's tinted light blue—that he opens up and places under my nose.

"Do it," he says harshly.

It doesn't sound like Scott's voice. I'm confused.

"Sssssscott, whattttarrreyoouuuu don t'me?" I can't even register how these words come out of me. My head is swirling. I feel the color blue turning to purple turning to brown, mud, black, oil, sludge washing over me. I am going to puke.

I puke.

I keel over. Motionless. I see his shoes. Are those Scott's feet? They are black, Converse? I've puked on them a bit. I hear him muttering, pissed off at this. I am able to gather myself for a minute and I stand up. I swing my arms. I think I'm yelling. I am moving like molasses. He puts my head in a hold. Now I realize it's not Scott. He is right back at me with the gel, right there under my nose. What's he doing to me? I am trying to muscle up adrenaline to help me save myself, but my head is spinning, and my vision is lobbing black spots. Large black spots. I can't see. My hearing goes. I faintly hear him. He clenches my neck harder, under my ears, a vice, two fingers, digging. I hunch my shoulders up in pain. He moves his hand around and places a thumb in the front of my throat, my trachea. I'm shaking. I am trying to pull myself, will myself to save me, but I can't. I surrender. He is squeezing tighter. It's painful. My brain is going to explode.

"Do IT!" he commands and grabs the back of my neck, pushing my nose into the capsule.

"Why?" I bellow. "Whhhhhhy? Jessssssusssss, wha the—"

"Do it!" he yells. He's pissed. His squeeze is tighter. I am losing. I am losing breath. I inhale through my nose, a huge sniff, so extreme that I snort. I feel the contents of the gel dusting my nostrils. I feel the bitter taste in the back of my throat.

I feel myself falling. I slide down. I'm down. My cheek is on the cold concrete floor. The SUV above me. The pitter-patter of rubber-soled shoes gliding away. The voice in my head said, *this was such a good plan.* My breathing slows. I am a lump. A cold, clammy, lump. I hear my heart beat.

And then I don't.

25

CHLOE? ROSE? GIRLS are you fighting? I need you to stop it. Scott? Are you there? Are you handling this? I feel all of them around me—feel their breath, their heartbeats—and I can smell them. There is chaos, that is clear, but I can't quite comprehend why I can't be there, but I am not here. I am somewhere.

Colorful, streaming narratives. Poetry.

Rose, my wonderful, beautiful, sensitive middle child. The black-haired beauty of the family. Black-as-night hair to match her black-as-night eyes. And her soul—well, that is dark too, but I know she fights it all the time. I know Rose. *I know her.* She has a hole in her that she is always trying to fill, and it will probably be that way for her entire life. She got it from me. Those holes are inherited. They are then passed on from one sad generation to the next, only to go bust or belly up at some point in midlife, and then restructured and reconfigured and passed on again. Very few of the holes get filled. They are left empty and open—

129

wounds that don't heal. With chronic but hidden pain, some are dangerously filled or wrongly filled with excess, covetousness, shallowness, sadness, self-pity. While others clog with loneliness.

But Rose was not the one I worried about, because those who have the hole to fill are usually preoccupied with the pursuit of filling it, and therefore preoccupied, and therefore fairly oblivious to the root cause of complete and utter despair. Rose will find her path and take it without an inch of concern for anyone else. She will do it on her own and probably give the rest of us the finger on her way out of town.

No, Rose is not the one I worry about.

Religious revelations. Reincarnation. St. Peter at the pearly gate.

Chloe is the one who sits like a monkey on my back all the time. Chloe bears down heavy on my shoulders, because, same as Atlas, she holds the whole world and all its problems, with judgment, on her shoulders, in turn putting all that weight on me. While heavy to me, that's a big burden for a teen, but she does it to herself. It is a pity too, because she is a stunner. She has the most gorgeous brown hair, with auburn highlights, and these giant, wide-set hazel eyes. She is probably the brightest of the three. Maybe Rose is as bright, but we'll never see this manifest in any way because she's not aware of it and will never, by any conventional measures, apply herself to anything that will prove this. But Chloe proves it on paper. She scores off the charts in everything she does. Her comprehension level is superior and her logical thinking, stellar. The problem with Chloe is that she gets herself bogged down with the often tedious practicalities of life. She frets over running out of cereal or milk. I mean, really. She acts like a crazed raccoon, always worrying about the family.

Because of this, Chloe ascertains the real deal. She wraps herself with the everyday duties because she is beholden to the truth—her truth—that it is only, and always, all about love. That one four-letter word that is so hard to get, grasp, handle, hold, and keep. That if, for a fleeting moment, you think you saw it at its finest and fullest, you are never quite sure. Much like the game of Kerplunk, so many other needles holding the marbles really determine the fate of pulling one needle. To even invest and investigate, experiment, give and take is a crapshoot. She never unwraps. This pains me.

That mystical light at the end of the tunnel.

Luna is my little peanut. So innocent. Lighter in body and soul than Chloe and most certainly Rose. She is almost blonde and with big brown eyes, matching many of Scott's traits. She is the charmer of the family. She does as she is told and acts the "good" girl to Rose's "bad" girl and the optimist to Chloe's skeptic. Luna's armor is dresses and ribbons (where Rose's is black jeans, boots and leather, and Chloe's is Brooklyn Boho). We all have our armor. Her sisters act as her enforcers, never really turning her against me but certainly sometimes keeping me from being closer to her. I get it. I haven't been the most attentive mother as of late. I have some issues. Luna has her magic. Luna's magic tricks will prevail. Luna is her magic. In the end, it will protect her.

As the heart stops and we die, the brain is thought to be flatlined and nonfunctional. However, there is growing evidence that in this state (as people pass away), there are markers of activity (beta, delta, and sometimes gamma waves) that emerge for a very short period.

I'm feeling restful. Finally at some peace. I'm in a church. I'm in the front pew. I'm focusing. Look where I am now? It's working. It's helping and I can feel it. Really. This is great. The ultimate feeling. I am sequestered to concentrate. I am going off the grid.

As people die and the parts of the brain that are ordinarily active during our day-to-day lives are no longer required and shut down, they enable the disinhibition of areas in the brain that are otherwise ordinarily not active and are inhibited in day-to-day life. This is what we are seeing with the emergence of those brain markers at the time of death. This disinhibition of these areas then seems to give people access to dimensions of reality that they ordinarily do not have in day-to-day life. This may be important from an evolutionary perspective, as they may not be needed until we reach death.

The voices fade. I can feel each one of them begin to fall away. Others step in to arrange me. I am being handled. I am being prepared for some kind of delivery.

I begin to fall away.

I fall.

There is little to no debate about when life ends. The Society for Post-Acute and Long-Term Care Medicine says "death has occurred when an individual has sustained either irreversible cessation of circulatory and respiratory function or irreversible cessation of all function of the entire brain including the brain stem."

BLACK. It's black.

BLACK.

26

I HEAR THE whir of the fans or some kind of motor humming in the background. It aids and abets my falling in and out of consciousness.

The last I remember, Scott is picking me up to head to a party. His father is letting him take their new Cadillac. Their tenth new Cadillac in less than five years. Representing the teamsters union at General Motors has its perks. This particular model is not due out until '78. Another perk—test-driving prototypes. The Eldorado—apparently "the only American luxury car in its class (or any car class) to be offered with 'Power Sliding T-Tops' that fold neatly inside the center-front roof," Scott banters with pride. It is obvious he has memorized exactly what his father said to him.

Cute, I think.

Tonight I am clear of Scott's house, his mom's quiet, glaring,

133

silent accusations, and his father's contemplative, pained avoidance. The plan is to pick me up at 8:00 p.m. sharp, and at 8:00 p.m. sharp, the cruiser pulls up in the driveway. Scott is exuberant, keeping the motor running, and with a skip in his step, he gallops up to and through the door and right into the shit storm of my family that night.

My mom and dad happen to be there (a rare sighting), fighting over Franky heading back overseas with the Marines for what my mother called "dangerous covert operations." I think he is going to Laos or Cambodia since the U.S. had pulled its troops from Vietnam. However, it's rumored we are still in Nam fighting, and my mother is over the top. It is a fierce fight between my mom, who is ready to throw her body over Franky to prevent his leaving, and my dad, who is telling my mom to mind her business.

While all this is unfolding, Franky is curled up in his bed, in his nice big, wood-paneled, shag-carpeted bedroom, spooning his high school girlfriend, Sherrie, while watching some dumb movie on a portable first-generation television with a taped up, strategically foiled rabbit-ear antenna. It doesn't matter how much fighting is going on. Franky is going to wake up one day and be gone again. He is the type of person who thinks he never owes anyone an explanation. This incites fury in those who need explanations; while those who don't, learn not to care. Explanations are knit into that family sweater and if you never provide any, you are not even part of the yarn.

Scott takes a deep breath in and raises his eyebrows with the *You ready to go?* look. When my mom throws the Waterford ashtray across the room, missing my dad's head by an inch, I give Scott the *Are you fucking kidding me?* look. Grabbing him by the coat and making a mad dash for the door, the last we hear on the way out is my mom shrieking at the top of her lungs, "Jesus Bob! It's like we are killing one off! Do you get that? Do you? Let's just go put *this* gun to his head right now! R-r-r-right now!"

This has happened twice before, and while it all ends up fine later, it is going to get bad—for a bit. The irony is that Franky probably has his hand up Sherrie's shirt and doesn't hear any of what is going on outside his door.

"Are you ready to go?" I hear Scott say. I thought I told him yes. 'Yes, Scott, yes!' Look at them. We can't stick around. *Why is he asking me this again?*

My own deep, labored snores wake me. My eyes pop open wide, searching for Scott. I hear my own voice in my head: *Yes, Scott, yes.*

There he is, sitting next to me, staring right at me.

"Grace," Scott says, "I need you to come to." He leans forward, snapping his fingers in my face.

I can't shake where I am or think I am. The humming gets louder. I hear other voices—no longer my parent's. There is a smell. *That* smell. That is first to awaken my senses. I can smell disinfectant, metal, lavender soap, witch hazel. I open my eyes. The crusts that had sewn them closed are now gone. Scott is sitting calmly and patiently. I'm not sure how much time has passed.

"They are telling me you can leave. To come home," he continues. I'm not sure he even cares whether I can hear or not, whether I am conscious or not. He is stating this now, right now, as if it is on his list to say and he needs an answer. I don't know the answer. I am shaking my head. To come to. To be in this room. To be present.

"What do you think," he says, not really asking.

My sticky, dry, and dusty mouth can not muster a peep. My lips are dead. I don't feel them. My brain is not motoring up. I'm drowning.

"I'll tell you what I think," Scott says, this time not so quietly but more firmly. "I think you cannot come home."

Sticky. Fuzzy. Dusty. Dead.

A slow churn, my stomach, not my mind. I vomit with a burp. With my head tilted to the right, the vomit flows out of the corner of my mouth and dribbles down my hospital gown. It's a putrid smell. Medicinal. Bile. It at least helps me to try to comprehend what Scott is saying to me.

"Your only option upon leaving the hospital is an inpatient program," he says while tapping a pamphlet on his knee. "I've selected one for you."

My mind begins racing at the same time I start falling away again.

"It's over, Grace. Over."

27

CHOKING ON MY saliva, pulling the words from as far back in my throat as I can feel, back where that vomit began its journey, I cough, and the words, however small, start working their way to my consciousness, delicately bold, however surprising, come barreling out, quietly but definitively.

I gasp.

"I want to live."

PART IV
Redemption
Vermilion Bay

28

"YOU SAW THOSE paw prints, did ya? Eh?" the nurse, Joey, nods to me. Joey is a local. She was a nurse for over twenty years in Winnipeg, the largest city, four-hours "close enough," to actually make a living. Then, when her family could no longer care for the cows and horses (which is how they made their living, selling one steer a year), she and her boyfriend Rob came to the rescue and moved back to the town of 1,200. Now 1,202.

Joey has anxious wiring, and with Rob taking over the primary farming chores, Joey needed more to do. So when the Vermilion Bay Rehab Center (Canadians call it as it is) was built, she showed up one day, put on a med jacket and started making rounds. Administration wasn't aware they had a new employee for six weeks and had to adjust her pay retroactively even though she never asked them to do so (also very Canadian on both accounts).

"Eh? Yeah. We have a pack. Must be the Alpha male. It's the

141

size of my forearm!" Joey exclaims with a cough, raspy, from the smoke breaks five minutes to the hour, every hour, outside in the -47 degree "weather." Joey is sprite but steel-like. Her forearm probably measures six to eight inches making that wolf, a gray wolf, by her calculations, about 130 pounds, and from hoof to head, standing upright, over seven feet tall—the largest non-domestic member of the dog family. In all forms of storytelling, from mythology to folklore—even embedded in our common languages—the gray wolf gets the bad rap. Because its population once neared the highest numbers of any other land mammal ever (after humans and lions), and because they are great hunters of large hoofed animals, it got itself whacked often. To the point of almost extinction until respective governments, by way of animal lovers, stepped in to save them. Since their species has survived over thirty thousand years, and they produced the lovely domesticated dog offshoots, they get a pass; only one in which we can manage and maintain them. Accordingly, the beaver colony that was here when I arrived, and has since been completely wiped out, isn't afforded the same reverence. Could it be the mane? The paw size? The peskiness? It's a blatant visual lesson, or warning, to the addicts, that as long as we are managed, we can stay.

I'm surrounded by my pack here. All sniffling. Running noses abound. It's all part of the detox. The body unloads the load. Anxiety. Irritability. Body pain. Tremors. Hungry. Not hungry. Starving. Sick. Throwing up everything. Throwing up nothing. The feeling of throwing up constantly. Diarrhea. Fatigue. Migraines. Double vision. Numbness in fingers and toes. Sweats. Sleeplessness. Sleepiness. Leg cramps. Cravings. Shivering. Muscle tension. Heart racing. Difficulty breathing. Tightness in the chest. Tremendous stress. Anxiety, did I mention that? If so, then up it to *body-rattling* anxiety.

The entire process takes anywhere from a few days to several years depending upon how long, how much, and what the fuck substance or substances one lets take hold of the controls.

"I'm hoping no one here has been dumping any scraps outside. That'll be enough to bring'em around. They got a nose, a smell. They can sniff a frozen dead frog out from two miles away, in good weather," Joey expounds, to me, but also the room of seven others, who pay her no mind because we are all sniffling, shaking, and convulsing. The wolf pack is not front and center in our minds.

She gives a nod to the "kid" (who is probably a local working off his halfway house time there as the janitor) to make sure there aren't any food droppings outside that'll draw the wolves in. Somehow he sees her nonverbal direction and makes his way to the door, his head hung so low and his outgrown sandy-brown, Justin Bieber-cut covering his face. His bangs are practically to his chin, a slight, straight nose peeking its way out, resembling an icebreaker on an empty-hulled ship. He is a mix between James Dean and a young Frank Sinatra. If he were on the streets of Paris or New York, he'd be swooped up to model, or to audition for a role in a commercial or indie Hollywood film. But here, close to the center of Canada, close enough to the North Pole to provide daylight eighteen hours in a day, he is simply another recovering addict. He slowly moves his cart to the window to check. In passing, I note a few tattoos on the inside of his arm. "Just breathe" at the top. Under that one, "Tomorrow is another day"; and under that is a heart and arrow and a name I can't make out. I want to tell him he shouldn't have bothered to try to remind himself. The next breaths, the tomorrows come, and go, whether you want them to or not.

"One hundred times more powerful than that of humans," Joey continues. "A wolf can tell, from the mere scent of another wolf, the age, sex, what level it is in the hierarchy, if it's been a parent, had pups, and even its personality."

Joey doesn't care whether we are listening, or is even interested. She would have told this to the air, to the spirits in the room. After all, she is of Cree ancestry, the largest of the First Nations in Canada. The Cree believe in a spirit world that surrounds us, which both protects and challenges us. In fact, in order to pass into adulthood, all Cree go off on their own for several days and fast until they have a vision—a "vision quest"—baptizing them into this world that is beyond.

"That blanket and peace pipe *you all* reference is figurative too," she enjoys reminding everyone. Whether it serves as her protection from all of us addicts, and our auras of disaster we bring to those wide-open expanses of purity, or if she really knows something more than the rest of us, she has certainly schooled us that we are not even close in evolving to any defined high state or being. In fact, because we are even there means we have wounded not only the flesh but the soul, of the clean carriage awarded to us upon entry into this physical sphere.

"Shame on you," she whispers often, because of what we had done to ourselves.

"The pack would have you off'd. They get rid of the sick, the weary, the weak link. Even the mothers," Joey says as she turns to me on that last line. I exhale a minor scoff. The irony that she smokes cigarettes is not lost on me. And the irony is not lost on her that we couldn't figure out she knows who each one of us is, for exactly the same reasons. Her comments are always a bit testy—her measuring, a level of presumption, judgment, at this point in our healing journeys—*and* possibly not allowed. Joey is Joey, who reports to Tina, who protects Joey.

Tina competes in *local* rodeos. That should be all I need to say to those who are familiar with local rodeos.

Local is emphasized because those who move up and on for show, ribbons and—least concerning—the money, do it for just that. But if you stay local, you win to claim your reign. You cement a place in legend, you hope. You make a mark. Right up there next to the fish tales of greatest catches.

Tina, originally from Minnesota, is head nurse but might as well be called Queen. Rarely saying a word, she gives you a look. Joey, doing all the mechanics, is Tina's enforcer. Together they keep the Center together and well centered.

"You don't have a problem, Grace," Joey says to me out of the blue.

"Excuse me?" I reply.

"Yeah, eh, you, I've seen'em come and go. You don't have that itch. You might be a G-D firecracker, but you don't have that chip. I can see it," she states. Without another thought, she returns to her daily duties.

"Wait . . ." I am interested in her take. If I have learned one thing in life, it is to leave it to those on the ground, who know by seeing what it's all about—Joey and the Queen.

"What, there's nothing more to say, really—" Joey says while shrugging.

"But . . ." I say, trying to keep her with me, on me.

"Look, do your time. Work with Bob. Get out. Get going. You're just wasting time. That's your choice," Joey says, cutting to the chase.

"But . . ." I am trying, trying to get something. Anything. The finality with which Joey says this, and the way she so confidently tells me, really, who I am, makes me feel mothered, cradled without her even touching me, in a way I never knew. I wish she had been my mom thirty years ago.

"No buts," Grace. "You're wasting time, and again, it's your prerogative. Come on. You got one moment of light between two, well, eh, unknown really, periods of total darkness," she pauses to let herself hack a cough forward. Wheezing on inhale to collect enough air for her finale.

"Let me put it in terms you Americans can understand— don't be such a pussy," she laughs with a cough, "get on."

29

THERE ARE APPROXIMATELY sixty-four thousand Alcoholics Anonymous ("AA") groups in the U.S. and Canada, with more than 1.4 million members. In comparison, worldwide, there are about 115,000 groups supporting more than two million members. In Australia there are only eighteen thousand members in roughly two thousand groups.

I blame religion. Escaping religious persecution, crossing an angry ocean on rickety ships, half of us in if not urine-drenched, then quite astute-smelling corsets, bloomers and layered petticoats. Viciously, we had to survive. We had to conquer what was expected to be a barren land to make sure we could pray our own way. It must have created the inherent pressure to drink and do drugs. No doubt. The prisoners sent down under seem to have acquired better adaptive instincts.

Scott found the one rehab center about a wolf pack's circumference (up to 1,200 miles to be exact) from civilization.

He was making sure I could not make it back—even on foot. Addicts can do amazing things. Achieve wondrous feats. There should be a chapter in the Guinness book of world records exclusively for addicts' mind-blowing endeavors. Besides the expansive terrain, the weather and temperatures sure to bury me above ground, and the predator that would find me a fitting appetizer, I certainly was not going to evade the Queen's eye nor Joey's suggested (and therefore imagined) spiritual Cree "wrap," which figuratively wafted through the air with an aura similar to burning sage in a house possessed.

Canadians take their rehab very seriously. They want you one and done, because in most cases, their government is usually paying for the rehab. I thought I'd end up at The Dunes of East Hampton. There were other possibilities—in California, the Cliffside, Wonderland, or the Meadows. Names such as Serenity, Promises, Reflections. Even any one of the seventeen Betty Ford Clinics would have been acceptable to me. Shabby chic couches that help you disappear, saunas to bleed the toxins, jacuzzis to fire up the circulation; fireplaces, real and working with cedar logs, and fabulous dancing flames to lick your wounds; essential oils for mind, body and soul to kindly rub away the scars, both real and imagined; bedding that engulfed you, held you close, kept you down for the night, in every room. These are the rehab Ritz' and Four Seasons.

Honestly, who wouldn't want to fucking relapse after staying at those places? It was a place to put Mom when she was acting up again. Or Dad, when a little too much scotch got to him after shady stock deals, taking him out of circulation of any financial dealings that might trigger the downfall of the family fortune. For addicts, with money, comfort comes ten-fold.

For those privy to how to game the system by scamming insurance plans and Medicare or Medicaid, these five-star facilities give drug-addled welfare queens and kings one shot at upper-crust care too. Similar to Hotels.com customers, there is always a separate wing for those who pay less or can't pay. At least they get the red-carpet treatment, once.

Regardless of the medical and insurance industry maneuvering it would have taken, which Scott would never have even entertained, I ended up at the Motel 8 of rehabs in the northernmost geographical area, with frozen tundra and a wolf pack to boot.

Vermilion Bay was originally a construction camp where railway workers were based starting back in 1881, to build what would become the Canadian National Railway. In 1903, a one-room school was built, and the township was first surveyed in 1906. The early 1900s also saw gold and soapstone mining on the southwest shore of Eagle Lake, with Vermilion Bay used as a supply center. The 1930s saw activity with the construction of the Trans-Canada Highway, and the 1940s were busy with activity in the forest industry. Tourist camps in the '40s. Granite quarries in the '50s. Then the fishing camps proliferated. Period.

The community is at the southern end for both Ontario Highway 105, which heads north to the town of Red Lake, and Ontario Highway 647, which heads northwest to Blue Lake Provincial Park. The Canadian Pacific Railway (CPR) transcontinental main line passes through the community, and while the CPR has a bulk forest products facility in the community, there is no passenger service.

There is one licensed radio station, CKQV-FM, which also focuses on the larger population centers of Kenora, Dryden, and Sioux Lookout.

Thank you Scott.

30

"ALRIGHT FOLKS, LET'S take a seat. Let's get going. Get your coffee and your healthy snack and let's get started," Joey says, loud enough for everyone to hear but soft enough to garner attention.

"Here," says a young man, mid-twenties, striking blonde hair, pulling out a chair for me.

"Oh, thanks," I reply, eyeing him cautiously. New. I don't remember seeing him before this meeting.

"Okay, yes, new faces in the room. Let's go around and introduce ourselves to them," says a different voice. It's the therapist, Bob. He always opens the meeting.

Introducing herself, Vivienne presents her story, the same way, the same voice, every time. Bob has to use his hand to wave her on to finish. There is always *that* person. After Vivienne, the summaries get shorter as the introductions work their way

151

around the circle.

"Grace," I say and pause.

"A bit more Grace?" Bob urges.

"No," I reply. "That's it." There is a moment of silence but not confusion.

"Alright then," Bob chuckles looking at the young man to my left.

"Um, yeah, Axle, um Ax, people call me Ax," the kid says. "Yeah, that's it."

Everyone gives him a nod. It's not expected to say anything more your first time in group. I can't remember what day it is. It doesn't really matter. The days blend. All we know is that it is another day sober and that's about it. The room has a winter-season chill because the heat can't get ahead of the weather, which rings in below zero, consistently, the wind-chill bringing it into the negative teens, negative twenties and sometimes thirties at night. Brutal.

At the same time, the chill keeps us awake, present, alive. The urge to climb into bed and bring the thin, insufficient (for a reason) covers up over your head is overpowering, but part of learning will power is learning not to do exactly that. You begin administering this will power with the smaller things and hope it has a ripple effect to the bigger things. One hopes.

"Alrighty then," Bob continues, "we are all on various steps. Does anyone want to share?" Vivienne's hand shoots up.

Though the original Twelve Steps of AA have been adapted over time, the premise of each step remains the same for all recovery programs that use a twelve-step model: Explore the steps in depth. See how others have applied the principles in their lives. Use them to garner insight into your own experiences. Gain strength. Hope for your own recovery.

The steps and their principles are these:

1. Honesty: After many years of denial, recovery can begin with one simple admission of being powerless over alcohol or any other drug a person is addicted to. Their friends and family may also use this step to admit their loved one has an addiction.

I am fucked up. There, honesty. But not from drugs.

2. Faith: Before a higher power can begin to operate, you must first believe that it can. Someone with an addiction accepts that there is a higher power to help them heal.

Zip, zilch, zero.

3. Surrender: You can change your self-destructive decisions by recognizing that you alone cannot recover; with help from your higher power, you can.

Hell no.

4. Soul searching: The person in recovery must identify their problems and get a clear picture of how their behavior affected themselves and others around them.

In my opinion, this is what drugs and booze help do.

5. Integrity: Step 5 provides great opportunity for growth. The person in recovery must admit their wrongs in front of their higher power and another person.

Break'em down to build'em up.

6. Acceptance: The key is accepting character defects exactly as they are and becoming entirely willing to let them go. Letting go of stress and grudges and cutting out intolerances, clutter and negativity to increase resilience. Meditate, exercise, focus on the positive, and surround yourself with positive and supportive people, to name a few.

I am here.

7. Humility: The spiritual focus of asking a higher power to do something that cannot be done by self-will or mere determination.

Repeat: I am here.

8. Willingness: This step involves making a list of those you harmed before coming into recovery.

Easy.

9. Forgiveness: Making amends may seem challenging, but for those serious about recovery, it can be a great way to start healing your relationships.

Not so easy.

10. Maintenance: Nobody likes to admit to being wrong, but it is a necessary step in order to maintain spiritual progress in recovery.

Hmmm.

11. Making contact: The purpose is to discover the plan your higher power has for your life.

No comment.

12. Service: The person in recovery must carry the message to others and put the principles of the program into practice in every area of their life.

Not going to happen.

No surprise in that two guys named Bill and Bob founded AA in 1935. Bill Wilson and Dr. Bob Smith believed that all problems were rooted in fear and selfishness. They believed that through the power of God and, by the way, following *their* "Four Absolutes," there is a cure. Those four absolutes are "absolute honesty, purity, unselfishness and love."

This, to me, hinges on the pervertedness of absurdity and guarantees a complete roadmap to failure because they are steeped in a basic prescription of, and for, morality (which didn't exactly go out the window but never existed in the history of mankind—like ever).

Add to that, it has to be executed through public sharing and confessions.

Barfing.

Now.

The Twelve Steps and the *fellowship* of AA were founded and designed around those principles. The purpose is to recover from compulsive, out-of-control behaviors and restore manageability and order to your life.

Routine. A lane. Railings.

It's a way of seeing that your behavior is merely a symptom of what is really going on. A check engine light that goes on in a car that forces one to investigate what's really going on under the hood.

I never once bothered to look into any light that came on in the car. That was Scott's job.

According to the American Society of Addiction Medicine, "Twelve Step facilitation therapy is a tried-and-true proven approach." Almost ninety years later people are still working the steps.

But it's anonymous, lacks reporting, and so there is no way to be sure it works.

People are encouraged to take an honest look at themselves, then deconstruct their egos and rebuild, little by little. The Steps encourage the practice of honesty, humility, acceptance, courage, compassion, forgiveness and self-discipline—pathways to positive behavioral change, emotional well-being and spiritual growth.

Does anyone want to give me a Hallelujah?

The Twelve Traditions are guidelines for healthy relationships between the group members and other groups.

Fail.

While the Twelve Steps were originally based on the principles of a spiritual organization, a lot has changed since 1935 and the word "God" has been replaced with "Higher Power." This is supposed to make it more accessible to everyone, regardless of their faith's traditions or beliefs. A Higher Power doesn't have to be God; it could be nature, the universe, fate, karma, your support system, the recovery group itself, medical professionals or whatever you feel is outside of, and greater than, yourself or your ego. What you believe to be a Higher Power is a very personal thing.

Being stoned is my higher power.

31

IN BED AT night, hours dragging on and on, I lie there think-ing. We have homework. It is to progress in depth and detail during the length of our terms. Mine is ninety days. I start a marking system on the wall to indicate the days to keep my mind sane. Check. Check. Check. When the Queen noted this, she brought me a calendar, with scenic, peaceful photos related to each month, to pin on my corkboard. I wondered, since we were in Canada, why the months from October to May were not all snow scenes. Joey came a few days later and replaced it with one exhibiting the twelve hottest delivery guys in Ontario. The Queen and Joey continue to switch these out in my room on a fairly regular basis, and I continue to scratch notches in the paint of the cinderblock wall.

Alone with my thoughts, thinking of my homework, I begin the breakdown. As is the plan. Par for the course. Breaking you down before building you up with good, decent habits to carry on until the final great plunge into total darkness. Whether one thinks that is death or relapse is unknowable, and personal.

The first homework assignment is to define violence. My guess is that they want us to understand that by abusing drugs, it is violence to oneself. I'm not comfortable writing something down off the top of my head without looking up the exact definition of violence.

"The intentional use of physical force or power, threatened or actual, *against oneself,* another person, or against a group or community, that either results in or has a high likelihood of resulting in injury, death, psychological harm, maldevelopment or deprivation."

Ah, there it is, *against oneself.*

I now can write what I think to be my definition of violence, to sincerely do the homework as asked, for my therapy session with Bob.

The definition of violence is, to me, to have to define it.

32

"GRACE," BOB SAYS, softly. I'm staring off into space. Our private sessions have been, up to this point, basic. Back and forth, this and that. Bob laughs off, dismissively, my short answer to the first homework assignment, calling me pedantic.

"Funny. I think the same of you," I reply.

Dr. Bob is not amused.

"Grace, to get anywhere, we have to start somewhere," he says.

"Where are we going? Where am I going?"

"You want to get better." Bob says, answering with an upward inflection. I'm not sure if it is a question or not.

"Scott wants me to get better," I reply.

"Better might not be the correct word. You want to be healthy, no longer with addictive habits," Bob purrs soothingly.

Trying hard not to shut me down.

"Scott wants me to be healthy," I murmur.

"You don't?" Bob asks.

"I don't think I was not healthy," I answer.

"Okay, Grace, okay. Let's go over your second homework assignment, which you very nicely handwrote. Things you remember from your childhood that might have served as a foundation to your propensity for addiction," Bob says as he draws out the final syllable, "nnnnn," keeping the floor so he can ease into the first memory.

"Your mother was told she had toxemia when pregnant with you, and she took diet pills to keep her ankles from swelling," Bob reads from a yellow pad I had been given to write on.

"Yeah, yeah, and when I was born, they had to spank me to start breathing. They'd slap my feet to wake me up as I preferred dozing off to nursing in my state of withdrawal," I reply with a laugh. "This really explains it all, doesn't it?"

"Yes, and then here, number two, you write that scotch was rubbed on your gums to soothe you while teething." Bob continues.

"Yes," I reply. What else can I say? I wrote these things.

Bob continues to read the list in the most measured, monotonous voice he can muster, and because I already know the content of the paper, I find my mind slipping away from the present, as I am transported to each memory.

At the age of four, when my parents had lively cocktail parties, I'd search the room, sniffing the drinks for my mother's Chivas Regal scotch on the rocks. When nobody was looking, I'd steal the glass, and take tiny sips from it in the hall closet.

At some scrawny age when I still took baths, I'd line up the Dixie cups and play bartender.

When I was six, the babysitter canceled, and instead of canceling their plans, my parents took me with them to Chicago's Playboy Club. A Bunny greeted us at the door. I was offered a Kitty Cocktail, I think maybe two, and surprisingly I passed out. Now in hindsight, I'm sure they were spiked to knock me out so my parents could carry on with their evening.

I drank my first beer in fourth grade. Robbie Wilder and I buried them between the baseball diamond and the fence in a grassy area of the schoolyard and guzzled them at recess.

I smoked my first cigarette with Tina Hunter. We stole the Newports (*Alive with Pleasure*) from her mother, Sonya, who was the first woman I knew to be divorced. She was a full-time school teacher, who paid mind only to her current boyfriend, whoever he was at the time.

I smoked my first joint, wrapped in strawberry-flavored rolling papers, with Shane Lynx on my way to school (me headed to fifth grade and he on his way to middle school).

I did my first hit of mescaline in seventh grade with giggly Simone Mulligan on an environmental studies canoeing trip.

I continued to do mescaline almost every other weekend throughout middle school.

I went into business with Lizzie Mazley, rolling single joints (behind the Jack-In-The-Box across the street from our middle school) to sell quite blatantly in the hallways every day when classes changed at the sound of the bell. We made a lot of money, which we either saved or bought all our friends drugstore-lip gloss and other makeup. We never got caught.

During middle school and throughout high school (appropriately named), I experimented with many other drugs, including those called "basement drugs" (made in some delinquent-wanna-be-chemist's basement).

In eighth grade, during one bad "trip" on "strawberry double-dose T" (THC), where I swallowed one and "gummed" the other (not attractive, as it clung like jelly to the top of my two front teeth), my friend Prudence overdosed. We were licking the flowers that had fallen off her wallpaper so that they'd stick when we put them back on the wall. She turned to me, laughed, and then the color disappeared from her face, moving its way down her body, a white sheet descending, the blood being drawn down like a pushed syringe, until her knees buckled and she withered to the floor. Like one of the flowers. (She lived; and yes, continued tripping.)

One grand ol' time in high school, maybe junior year, maybe senior year, at a nondescript party in a well-appointed basement (pool, foosball, ping-pong, etc.), I tested my limit without any awareness I was testing it. I did four or five different drugs, washing it all down with alcohol. Vodka? Beer? I can't recall. Weed. A quaalude. Chased the dragon with H. I think the coke was last to wake up, so I was able to be alert enough to drive home.

The next day, I was in tears after the wrath of my dad. He had woken up to find the car parked with its back tires on the sidewalk. As I sat in the kitchen sniffling, he grabbed the wooden-handled kitchen knife and slammed it on the table.

"If it's so bad, just end it all right now," he raged. I continued to cry, thinking to myself, as I can recall so few memories from so many years ago, *Why would I want to do that?* He was the one making me miserable. My life was always fine until I got caught or until I did something my dad didn't want me to do. But it didn't make sense for me to end my own life. Maybe it had been a projection of what he wanted for me. I don't blame him. I gave him grief.

I remember one time coming home to all my clothes thrown from the second story window of my room. I can't remember what I did then to elicit getting kicked out of the house, but it must have been fairly bad.

I don't think it was when I took his new Corvette for a joy ride at the age of 13.

I don't think it was when I accidentally burned the back shed to the ground while playing with matches.

I don't think it was when I partied with friends on his boat, in his house, in his yard, or at his cottage.

I was beaten up three times by the boys in grade school. One time they shoved a snowball so far down my throat, I passed out. Another time they tied me to a tree and whipped me with sticks. The last time they followed me in a mob all the way home from school, pushing and shoving me to the ground, kicking me when I was down, grabbing me by the hair to make me get back up and walk again.

Once, an elderly woman, who came to babysit when my parents went on trips, drank from a bottle of their scotch and passed out. So I drank the rest and passed out next to her.

Another time, I was so angry at my dad for yelling and punishing me, I started punching myself in the eye. I wanted to give myself a shiner to prove he was abusive. I wanted to get him in trouble. It didn't work. I remember wondering precisely how hard someone had to get hit to get a black eye. It seems to happen without any effort when someone else is throwing the punch.

In my early twenties, my mother came clean to tell me that she basically gave me up to her mother so that her mother wouldn't be lonely. "My issues" were due to a sense of abandonment from an early age, especially after her mother, my Nana, died when I was seven.

Violence is intimate. Violence is most easily recognizable if blatant. The black eye. The bleeding, swollen lip. Broken bones are easily excused as accidents. The violence, most often undiscovered, buried, propagated, and proliferated, is invisible, a silent gas, seeping from one generation to the next generation.

Gosh, Bob. This was fun!

33

"THE NEXT ASSIGNMENT is to apologize. Make a list of those to whom you feel apologetic toward," Bob says as he readies himself to leave.

"Say you're sorry . . . to whom?" I ask, sitting comfortably, relaxed. I have nowhere to go.

"People you've harmed, mentally, emotionally, even physically," Bob chirped as he looked at me, wondering why I wasn't totally comprehending the assignment. I stared at him a long beat before the words so easily fell from my mouth.

"What if they're dead?"

34

THE LAST PART of the assignment is to show your vulnerabil-
ity while at the same time exhibiting the behavior to continue to
build trust. To do this, it is suggested to write down a secret. Tell
the group something you've never told anyone.

(Scott ran the red light.)

35

"I AM NOT a victim," I demand Scott acknowledge on a mandatory phone call Bob arranges because I stopped participating in the exercises.

Scott is silent.

"I made it to day sixty-eight. I do not need ninety days to realize that this place is pulling me somewhere I do not want to go," I reply, anger beginning to percolate. "A place you don't want me to go, Scott!"

Silence.

"Revealing a secret, Scott! Do you hear me?" my voice is rising. My chest is filling up with destructive air. "Our secret," I scream, blowing out. "A fucking painful, damaging secret that would change everything Scott! Everything! One secret!" I throw the phone down so I can punch an office window. It spiders but does not break. Eyeing a vase, I decide it's good enough. I send

169

it flying. Broken glass breaks the silence that I alone "hear" from Scott. Next up, a flying chair. I sever one chair leg from its seat. Brandishing it the same way Pam's brother, Johnny, man-handled the baseball bat so many years ago. My sword, I wield it mightily. I am my anger in physical form. The confusion enhances the circle of chaos. That surge of adrenaline, superb and so underrated. The earth-shattering sound of silence to bring it all to a head. Within seconds, power and control travel, like a current moving along a live wire, on its mission to reach the most receptive, chosen recipient. The one worthy of a greater need to survive, at all costs, Bob.

He is standing way too close, waiting for me to move away so he can pick up the phone that I threw to the ground. I stay as still as a predator awaiting my prey. I can first feel, and then smell, his breath on me. It is sour. It is a quick breath. He is nervous but trying to compensate for this by looming over and around me, as if this will somehow force me to cower. Instead, instinctively, I pull my shoulders back, puff my chest out, and barely bump him hard enough to make him lose his balance. Then, I slowly move past him, behind him, so he has to watch me from the corner of his eye. Narrowly beyond his reach, I turn to make sure he does not leave his back to me as he is turning to make sure he does not leave his back to me.

It felt good to fuck with Bob. It felt beyond the human sphere of emotions to play my final card with Scott. To release years of guilt, contempt, and resentment for something he did. *He did.* I carried it. I covered for him. I bore the breaking point.

It was exhilarating while it lasted.

Joey is in the doorway, watching. She puts her head down and looks at the floor. She does not make eye contact with me because we both know what she is thinking—she's heard every word. She doesn't need to confirm this.

Bob leans down and picks up the receiver. He clears his throat, mental anguish written all over his face, his hands are shaking. He says, "Hello, um, err, Mr. O'Doyle? Geez, yes, so sorry to bother you. Is this a good time?"

***

After summarizing the point to which I had progressed before the sudden and complete regression, Bob lays out the zero-tolerance laws of the land.

"For Grace to get past this, she has to participate. I can work out the throwing of the chair—well, the broken glass. Repair expenses, naturally, will be added to your invoice, I'm sorry to say," Bob mumbles while moving his mouth away from the phone, swaying it back and forth, creating an audio distortion, oscillating in and out, like a pendulum.

I imagine Scott's growing agitation. Pushing his chair out from the table, away from his newspaper, stomping into a room with the girls out of earshot, even though there would be nothing to hear because Scott would have nothing to say, as usual. "Pissed off" to Scott was typically hardly a tilt of the head.

Bob's voice falls off, inviting Scott to interrupt.

Scott remains silent.

"Um, so, well, if you'd like to, well, in order for Grace to stay, she has to complete the assignments," Bob wills himself back into the call, taking the lead, after Scott's silence encourages him to lean into what he knows—his job. I observe Bob pushing down a grip of threat. Scott's silence continues to pierce the call like a dog whistle at the highest training caliber; one the human ear could never register.

"It's fairly simple. Two-fold," Bob gives an ultimatum. He drops the bomb, not knowing he, himself, just closed the deal. Bob has not a clue the O'Doyles don't *do* ultimatums. I shake my head at Bob's lack of strategy. I picture Scott's head now tilting back straight, staring out the window, listening more intently for the next pearl dropping from Bob's stinky-ass mouth. Sliceable silence.

"Grace has to make a list and walk through and proceed to execute her apologies. This is a mandatory step in this—"

"THEY'RE FUCKING DEAD YOU IMBECILE!" I yell from my dingy, soiled chair in his office, where I've resigned myself during this dismal escapade. I can't hold back. I can take stupid for so long. And then I cannot! Take! Stupid! His assistant comes to the door, standing behind Joey, with a look of fear on her face. Joey doesn't flinch, her arms folded in front of her. She is looking me right in the eye. Bob waves the assistant away. I picture Scott, maybe cracking one quarter of a smile. Maybe?

"Um, errr, yes, well, you can hear Mr. O'Doyle," Bob's voice cracks, a bit of a pleading tone. "Ummhuh," high-pitch, Bob continues, "the last assignment, the final, is to break down barriers to vulnerabilities. To reveal, to study, to confess, well, confess is a strong word, perhaps too strong, but you get the idea, in a non-religious way, to reveal so that one can, well, to then build." Bob is stumbling but he pulls himself together. He keeps one eye on me, to make sure I do not pounce, verbally, and quite possibly even physically, and he continues to finish his sentence.

"To reveal, perhaps a burden, to relieve one of a burden, perhaps a, a, well, for lack of better words, a secret. I guess from what I can deduce from this unexpected, very unfortunate and really, quite debilitating outburst of Grace's, uh-hum, your secret perhaps?"

***

"The list. The condescension."

Silence.

It was going to be a long trip back. Scott flew into Minneapolis where he rented a car and drove seven and half hours due north to pick me up. We were retracing his steps.

"To apologize," I emphasize. We have to start a conversation about this at some point and with seven plus hours and a flight back east in front of us, to me at least, we had nothing but time.

But I am met with silence which continues for what seems like eternity. I am contemplating getting out of the car. Always black and white thinking with me. No middle. It is as if Scott reads my mind and clicks the lock button on the doors. It's almost painful, the distrust, the control.

"Pam. De—"

"Okay," Scott interrupts abruptly but quietly. "Enough."

"You know I would never . . . I'd never ever say—"

"Grace."

"But you have to know—"

"Grace. I said enough."

Scott glances my way from the corner of his eye. I can tell by the look, he *did not* know this. He never did. This is, and always has been, the thorn in his paw.

I am that thorn.

He sees me as a weak link. It makes me uneasy. It has always made me uneasy. I feel sick, sitting on the blade of anxiety at all times. Possibly why I indulged in numbing myself to oblivion.

The road ahead blurs. I see scenes flashing. Moments play as jump cuts. Scott—that night in the garage. The side of the car. The drug forced on me. *Was that him? Left for dead. Was that him? Have I been willing myself to be out of the picture all this time? Nothing more than aiding him?* He had always taken care of things. He was raised that way. The family knew how to *take care* of things. I don't trust what is behind me, and I certainly don't trust what is in front of me.

I have no other options. No other choices. I have to forge on. This is all I can do.

We drive in silence. We fly in silence. Together we stay silent. We will stay silent. Together.

36

EXPERT ESCAPE ARTISTS and incredibly destructive, the wolf is built for travel. Long legs, large feet, lean, deep, narrow chest, armor for its constant on the move trajectory. Keen senses, large canine teeth, powerful jaws. The ability to pursue prey at forty miles per hour equips the wolf well for a predatory way of life—covering up to 1,200 square miles of territory.

Wolves *usually* live in packs, *usually* a family group consisting of an adult breeding pair (the alpha male and alpha female) and their offspring of various ages. Each wolf has its own distinct personality. A dominance hierarchy is established within the pack, which helps to, *usually,* maintain order. The alpha male and female continually assert themselves over their subordinates, guiding the activities of the group. The female *usually* leads in the care and protection of the pups. The male provides the food and in doing so, decides location. Both are *usually* very active in attacking and killing prey, but not always. Sometimes, the kill is conducted alone. The pups, after a diet of regurgitated meat for six to nine weeks, when old enough, train to kill by luring local dogs into the forest with their playful yelps, "come hithering" the domesticated, fun-hungry distant relatives, who were smart enough to adapt for three squares and a warm cushion but not smart enough to eliminate their desire for play, even if dangerous.

Wolves communicate with one another by visual signaling (facial expression, body position, tail position), vocalizations, and scent marking. Howling helps the pack stay in contact and also seems to strengthen the social bonds.

The pups reach adult size at about ten months. After a few years in the pack, most leave to search for a mate, establish a new territory, and even start their own pack. One who stays with the pack might eventually replace a parent to become the breeding animal (alpha).

Wolves cover twelve miles or more in a day, hunting mostly at night, especially in areas populated by humans, when the weather is warm. Main prey are deer, elk, and the like, which they chase, seize, and pull to the ground. Beavers and hares are fair and easy game. Some wolves even fish for salmon. A large percentage of the animals that wolves kill are the young, the old, or those in poor condition. After making a kill, the pack gorges, devouring seven to twenty pounds per animal, reducing the carcass to hair and a few bones. Then the pack moves on, looking for another meal.

Sometimes, when necessitated by various circumstances, unusual conditions, or unexpected uncertainties, wolves will turn on each other, or on one member of the pack, and kill. This thins the pack of a contributor to their resources, but it is also a natural and motivated way to secure survival.

PART V
Rebirth
Jeffersonville, New York. One Year Later.

37

"OKAY, SO HERE. I've marked two hundred feet from the target," Scott says to Rose. The breeze is starting to kick up, a godsend to keep the bugs at bay, which can be brutal this time of year up at the country house.

"Okay." Rose.

"We'll start with the .22," Scott says. "I left the Ruger auto at home. Along with the .38 Special. We have enough here to start. I've got all the ammo there. We can bring the Big Boy out later if we want or—"

"The Beretta. I dig the Beretta." Rose interrupts enthusiastically. "Bring the Glock too. Let me give her another chance. A little more love."

"Ah, atta girl. Good spirit. So, um, okay well, we have to move up then. Like, well, to seventy-five feet. So, yeah, hold on," Scott says as he contemplates the new set up.

Scott turns his baseball cap around. Rose has her hair in a clean, tight ponytail. She's wearing her glasses. She looks prim, fresh. Refreshed.

"Okay, let's go here, set up," Scott says as he moves to the area with his backpack loaded with ammo, targets, measuring binoculars, and his large plastic Gatorade bottle full of diet ice tea.

"Leave the rifles there. We'll come back." Scott.

"What about the cone?" Rose asks.

"Um, yeah, leave it." Scott clocks the orange cone, meant for the road, to serve as a warning to stop for anyone coming or going once shooting begins. "We'll be closer to the target now."

Rose takes off her jacket and stretches her arms to get ready. She grabs the headphones to protect her ears and the safety eye goggles that fit easily over her square dark frames. She breathes in and out through her mouth a few times.

"All right, you want to load it or do you want me to?" says Scott, referring to the clip. "We'll start with the Glock."

"Um, you can, if that's okay." Rose.

"Sure, no problem," Scott says, his face gently lighting up. He's absolutely so happy to be with Rose, to finally be sharing this time.

"Luna? Where's Luna?" Scott inquires.

"She's in her room playing," Rose replies. "Dolls again. Witch and Baby Ghost. She's not letting that go."

"Yeah, um, a bit ol', but I guess—" Scott mumbles.

"It's okay." Rose says. "I asked her to come, but she's fine. She's okay."

"Hmm." Scott. "Yeah. Alright, let me see you set up. Keep the lock on."

"Like this, yes, this eye is my strong one," Rose says as she strikes an impressive stance, a pose. Scott smiles proudly. As usual, he gives a few more pointers. They pass the gun back and forth. Rose listens, watches, mimics.

"You'll do the first ten rounds, and we'll switch—" Scott says.

"Yeah, yeah, I want to switch. Do five on each side," Rose says.

"That's right. You are my ambi," he beams, referring to her ambidexterity that provides an advantage in sports. "You were always great at sports. That's for sure. In truth, your aim is better with your right eye, your weaker eye, right?"

"Yeah, maybe, we'll see, right? Been a bit."

"Alright, here we go. Yeah, you do ten and then we'll mark your hits, and I'll do the next round, and we can decide if we want to move back there to the rifles."

"Yeah."

"Okay, Luna is inside, right? Your mom—" Scott asks.

"Yeah. I, yeah, I don't give a shit." Rose says as she places her eye behind the sight to practice her set up. Scott gives Rose a knowing smile. Rose smirks.

Things return to normal. It was just a blip. The receding last ripple of the pebble thrown into the pond. Soon to be forgotten. Phrases such as "It's all behind us now," and "One day at a time," or "The future is out in front of us," come to mind.

All true.

Merely because they are all true doesn't mean you believe them.

A year of my own rehab is working. Understanding it is going to be a lifetime of conscious diligence. I certainly hope I enjoyed the ride while it lasted because even though leaving the roller coaster is better for me in the long run, certainly the future of flatness, flatlined feelings, is hard to swallow. What I see in front of me helps me accept it.

We had bought a mighty piece of land in upstate New York. About three hours from the city. It is a blessing in many ways. For my health. Nature is my new high. For those who know, it's fairly hard to replicate the real "true love"—the high from drugs.

For once, I see a peaceful road in front of me. I feel the demons, the sadness, and the guilt that has crawled up and harbored into a corner of my consciousness far less often. I am learning to live the light between the two periods of darkness— this light that is life.

While the trust factor between me and the girls is going to be a long process, I am learning to accept, not push. Their relationships with their dad are stronger and more meaningful than ever; possibly at my expense, but that's a selfish thought. What choice did they have? I put them in those situations. Their anger at me aided in their survival, their joining forces. Their contempt has not fully retreated. Oddly, Scott did, and continues to do, nothing to aid in this recovery. I'm aware he thinks I brought this on myself and that it will heal at a natural and organic progression, if even at all. I'm not sure I am in a place to easily accept this. I still don't know how to handle it or that it is within my power to figure it out. Powerless. *There, Step 1. I'll give you that, "Bob."*

While the girls have many things in common with Scott, the highlight, the one bond that surpasses the rest, of cooking together, biking, birdwatching, surprisingly, is marksmanship. Scott gathers his encased, locked guns and a backpack organized with ammo and other supplies. The four of them head out down the private road to the target area, taking turns, from varied distances, in different stances, shooting. A full afternoon of activity. Rose usually leads the team. She is a sure-shot, often surpassing Scott in points. She loves the new Glock but still favors the Beretta.

"I admire its kick-back," she recently proclaimed at dinner about the Glock, "but the Beretta is my baby. I like the feel of steel. It really lets *you* know you're holding it. Strong. You have to be strong."

Chloe is not here this weekend. She finally got her wish to "get away," with her boyfriend . . . *to Brooklyn.* She spends the very minimum of time, if any, with us. When she did shoot with Scott this past year, what she lacked in teeth she made up for with skill and precision. Luna usually spends more time dancing around them than paying attention to Scott's instructions. Luna shoots and she comments on the sounds, the music it all makes, from the ruffling of getting the .22 set up in her hands, leaning against the tree, to the pull back on her little finger, to the click of the trigger and the kick of the gunpowder pushing the bullet. She hears it all in musical notes.

It is the perfect day for a bike ride. The wind is light, the air brisk. Autumns are pure heaven up here in Jeffersonville. The period of time when one last blast of warm, balmy weather descends, stirring the past summer's glimmers of tranquility to the surface of one's memory. What we used to call the Indian Summer.

Scott had reminded me earlier that if the cone is in the road, they'll be shooting from the farthest mark and to stop and shout out my approach. I ready myself to ride down the hill, avoiding the ferocious rooster that has always had it out for me. I fend him off with a stick, or whatever is near, to protect me from his projecting mass charging at me claw-first. He might be king of his twelve hens and his roost but not me. Not today. It is a gorgeous day, blue-blue sky, a scatter of clouds providing deep contrast, chickadees wafting in flight across the pond to one of the many feeders we have spread out on the land, and the blowing breeze conducts the trees in harmony. The leaves have started to turn color, a complement to the rhythm of nature's choreography.

I count my blessings:

Chloe

I hope she's happy now. Brooklyn appears to suit her. Her

guy seems fairly nice.

Luna

My sweet, sweet magical baby. Such an imagination. I left her playing pretend with her dolls. I suppose her way of coping. Adolescent self-induced, subconscious therapy. I catch a glimpse of her in the window, rocking her doll.

It's okay, there, there. Don't cry. I know Mama's been away . . . gone. Here now but still gone, yeah, sad. I'm your mommy now. I'm going to take care of everything. You'll see. Everything will be alright.

Scott

Scott. Love or convenience? Love disguised as convenience. There's gotta be something there. Or we wouldn't have stayed in it. So I am thankful but wow, the choices we make when we are so young and dumb and the paths those choices take us on, and why we end up staying on. By choice? Out of necessity? Lack of other options—and if they even presented, what stops one from taking them? And then, eventually, too late to leave? Too old? Tired? No other ways out?

Rose

She's a pea in that same pod. So tough. Distant. Enforcer, no less. I see them from a distance setting up to shoot. No cone in the road. I get set up, aware that I will have to pedal hard downhill to pick up speed for the steep uphill climb beyond the dip, making it to our property gate with the least amount of pedaling effort.

My health

The only thing I want to feel right now is the wind through my hair. The smell in the Autumn air at its best—burn piles from afar, the instant aromatherapy from the pines and cedars, and the comfortable wrap of the light, heat from the sun acting as a permanent press cycle to the former dank, dewy air of the night. It is all here. All before me. Right here in front of me.

For this one moment, I am more at peace than ever before. For this one moment I believe all those cliches—"It's all behind us now," "One day at a time," "The future is out in front of us." Maybe even "Just breathe," and "Tomorrow is another day." For one moment . . . this is it. This is the feeling I was forever in search of. It is right here, right now. I feel it. One moment; it feels like heaven.

My life.

38

WHEN I WAS younger, my friends and I did what was called a Cakewalk at a local elementary school community fundraising fair. We were all stoned, of course, and the thought of winning a cake was tantalizing, although we never thought any of us would win. We were not winners in that way, in any way, ever.

The Cakewalk is a big circular path demarcated with numbers on paper taped to the ground. These numbers are also on pieces of paper in a box at the Cakewalk Table. The table is lined with donated cakes and pastries and pies of all sizes and shapes, packaged in all sorts of old and odd containers never intended for return (as opposed to the Tupperware circuit, where the collection of Tupperware makes its way from living room parties—where it's a duty to make a substantial purchase to help a Welcome Wagon neighborhood mother—to the cabinet, to each other's houses and back again).

Music played loudly from a big black nondescript boombox,

plugged into a very long, heavy-duty extension cord, also taped to the ground, which snaked its way into the school, keeping a school door ajar—forcing someone's aunt or grandmother to keep watch for hoodlums, who vandalized the school (being me and my friends, or Scott—who I had not met yet—and his friends). Several volunteers worked the Cakewalk Table: one to start and stop the music with a push of a button, one to pull the number on paper out of the box and maybe a few more to guard the cakes.

It is also a little-known fact that the Cakewalk was a pre-Civil War dance originally performed by slaves on plantation grounds. No one then knew this. Things are carried on and brought forth through tradition without any thought. Call it living. And that is what we did. For a total time of fifteen, maybe thirty minutes, after having waited in line for over an hour (buzzed), we made it on the circle. We proceeded as one person, in gaggle formation, around the circle. We were having a blast. Walking when the music played, dancing, acting silly, linking arms, pulling, pushing, hanging on. When the music stopped, we'd note our number and wait to hear if it was called.

I had never won anything in my life up to that point. But we won six times! Six cakes! We got to choose! We could barely carry them to the playground to dig in and eat them. We wobbled as we balanced two cakes each, in poorly packaged containers, to an open space over by the Cheesebox, a cement structure with cut out holes to look like Swiss cheese. While a playground staple, it inadvertently was a bully's dream haven enclosure in which to inflict torture and harm. This use, so prevalent, was soon "outlawed" by concerned parents of the next generation, and all Cheeseboxes were demolished. They were written into 70s toy history lore along with the pet rock, miniature seahorse families from Tiger Beat magazine, Sting-Ray banana-seat bikes with metallic handlebar tassels and clanky bike bells, Chia pets, and the Smiley face.

Elation was the feeling. The first taste of having "my cake

and eating it too." We were over the moon. We'd won. We'd won at something. The misfit, unmatched, latchkey kids of the neighborhood were in heaven for a minute. One minute. It felt great. We were winners.

Not everyone who drinks is an alcoholic or who does drugs is an addict. Sometimes, one indulges for recreation. Sometimes it's solely about participating. Feeling good. Maybe even winning a cake.

***

This is the same feeling I have now. The paranoia about Scott has subsided, which was probably a side effect after he got me out of rehab. With Vermilion Bay behind me for good, in my rearview mirror, I now realize I am being given a second chance. It is just taking some time.

A second chance.

39

"OKAY, YES, GOOD. Feet are good," Scott helps Rose adjust.

"Here?" Rose.

"Um, well, let me get behind you to help your arms get a little . . . more . . . and here," Scott mumbles, positioning himself for Rose's best shot. The Glock is not consistent, and there's no scope, not even a red dot mount. "Never a good one in a hurry; can't release safety fast enough. Um, yeah, and like the slide, yup, here. Can't ever understand, yeah, postal grip, macho shit, right?"

Rose nods as his breath moves her neck hairs, giving her a tingling sensation.

"When you go to pull the trigger, aim low, because the muzzle is gonna rise and shoot high. And loose but firm arms," Scott says as he leans into Rose. He then whispers in her ear, "You catch my drift?"

193

This she hears.

***

"Now little Witchy, here you go, use this," Luna says to her doll as she hands the doll the .38 Special. She had picked it up off the shelf that morning when Scott decided not to take it outside to shoot with Rose.

"It will help protect you . . . from all the bad guys," Luna says as she cradles the witch doll, putting the gun in the witch doll's raggedy arms. "Baby Ghost can show you how . . . see this?"

***

"What's this?" Chloe asks her boyfriend after sorting through the closet to make room for a new organizer system. She holds up a locked box. She knows what's inside.

"Ahhh, we live on this edge of protection, self—" he replies.

Chloe stares at the box.

"Hey, it's no big deal. We'll only use it if we need to."

Chloe tilts her head hearing a distant howling. She squints her eyes as if that will make the sound more decipherable. Chloe looks up from *that* box and stares out the window. Feeling a pinch in her heart and then as if something is literally sucking her consciousness, her blood pressure drops, and a vision of her mother comes to her.

***

"Okay, ready, straighten your arms, right, okay, let's, yup, finger, safety unlocked?" asks Scott.

"Yup!" Rose says.

"Together?" Scott asks, a twinkle in his eye, a smile on his lips, not seen since, well, hell, who can remember.

"Hell yeah! Why not!?!" Rose bellows, although she looks slightly weary, possibly uncertain, for once, as her eyes corner to the left at her father, straining to catch any other form of non-verbal communication, as she follows his orders. She breathes in with uneasy control, stiffens up like she is turning into stone as she holds her breath in, and as she prepares to pull the trigger, not as she was trained, she closes her eyes.

***

Off in the distance, Luna hears a howl. She cocks her head sideways, pausing. As if receiving a message, she moves the .38 down the dresser to the end, pointing the nozzle away, as her dad had trained her. She hugs her witch doll close, pats Baby Ghost on the head, and looks out the open window into the rustling trees.

"That's right Witchy, pull this, like this, when you need to," says Luna in a low whisper, as if Baby Ghost is speaking. "It makes everything okay. A . . . like . . . new kind of magic."

***

"Ahhhhhh," I howl. I take off down the hill, the wind in my face, in my hair. Free. Finally free.

40

FIRE.

41

CRACK.

42

WHACK.

43

THUD.

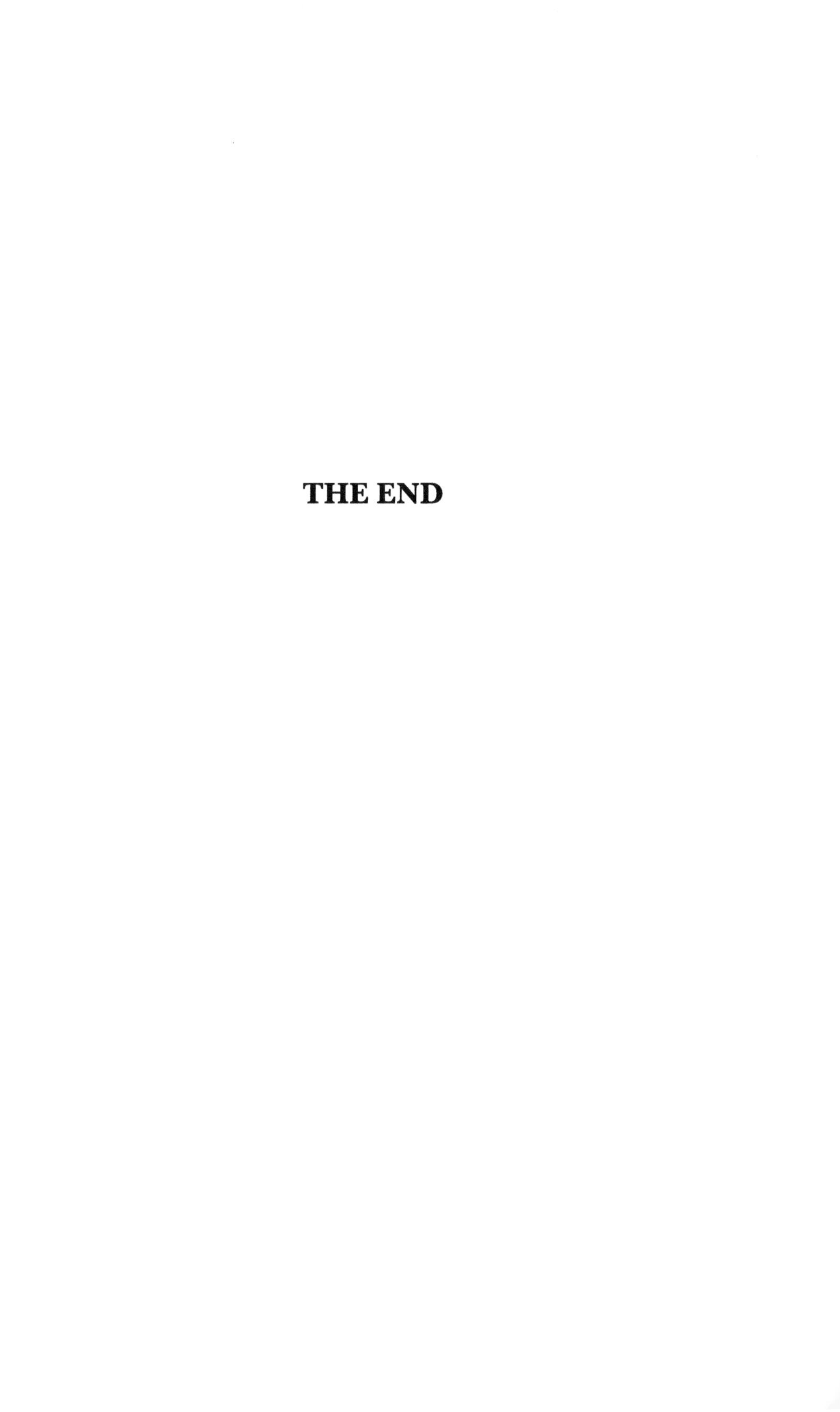

THE END

Acknowledgments

As always, Samantha Sewell for being my editor and designer, fellow-artist and friend. Charlie who is a guiding light, and at times frustrating, but always eventually, enlightening in surprising and unconventional ways. Raquelle Sewell who may never read any of my books but has always been supportive. My amazing beta readers and their detailed and honest input: Marilyn Agrelo, Andrea Brecia, Laurel Brett, Barb Ulmer Guest, Patty Freud, Susan Howard, Heather Ogilvie, Jake Raddock, and Catherine Ryan. Thanks to my granddog Wanda who is the best listener and helps me filter all my ideas. And, last but never least, to all my ghosts, still, who keep me company, often whispering in my ear, while writing.

Research References

Alternatives to Abstinence: A New Look at Alcoholism and the Choices in Treatment, By Heather Ogilvie Stone, 2002

Addicted To Bang: The Neuroscience of the Gun, By Steven Kotler, FORBES, December 18, 2012

Beginner's Guide to Guns, By John Adama, Self Defense Guides - Prepared.com, Updated September, 2023

Confessions of a Liberal Gun Owner, By Justin Cronin,, The New York Times, January 27, 2013

Dangers of Mixing Heroin and Meth, The Recovery Village, Updated May 4, 2022

Explaining the Basics and Exploring the Principles (and Everything in Between), The Twelve Steps of Alcoholics Anonymous, Hazelden Betty Ford Foundation, March 20, 2019

Living with Wolves, By Nikki Kolb, Catapult Magazine, January 13, 2023

"Speedballing": Mixing Stimulants with Opioids, Micromodule, Florida Department of Children and Families, MyFLFamilies.com, Florida Alcohol and Drug Abuse Association (FADAA), JBS International

Tranq Dope: Animal Sedative Mixed with Fentanyl Brings Fresh Horror to U.S. Drug Zones, By Jan Hoffman, The New York Times, January 7, 2023

Uniform Declaration of Death Act, The Society for Post-Acute and Long-Term Care Medicine, 1980

Vermilion Bay, Ontario, Multiple scouting visits + Wikepedia. org

What Are the 12 Steps of Recovery? By Buddy T., verywellmind.com, Updated on November 10, 2022

Wolf, Britannica.com

Your Brain at the Moment of Death, By David Levine, PROTO. LIFE, Aug 4, 2022

About The Author

 *The Hole in the Rabbit* is Amy Sewell's second thriller fiction novel. Pyschothriller *Pocket 8s*, her first, debuted in 2022. A published author, her nonfiction books include *The Mad Hot Adventures of a Documentary Filmmaker* (Hyperion, 2007) and *She's Out There! The Next Generation of Presidential Candidates* (LifeTime Media, 2009). Sewell is also a filmmaker best known for award-winning, audience-favorite MAD HOT BALLROOM. Other films include WHAT'S YOUR POINT, HONEY?, BLINDSPOT and SHAKE THESE BONES. Sewell has started her next book, *The Fence*, following two Gen Z sisters' sudden exile from persecution when the United States turns from democracy to dictatorship. Sewell resides in NYC with her husband of 30+ years, enjoys admiring her 20-something daughters with all they do, and is madly in love with Wanda, her rescue granddog.

Other Books
by Amy Sewell

Pocket 8s
She's Out There!
The Mad Hot Adventures of a Documentary Filmmaker

www.ingramcontent.com/pod-product-compliance
Lightning Source LLC
Chambersburg PA
CBHW071104100726
47908CB00008B/2263